Codes &
Decodes

JOHN KLAWITTER

DoubleSpin

Copyright © 2013 John Klawitter

All rights reserved.

ISBN:1938674073
ISBN-13:978-1-938674-07-5

DEDICATION

To my brothers, the Old Spooks & Spies,
Who came through with me
when we were all young and brave and foolish.
I salute you all, I thank you for your principles,
your craft, your sense of humor and
the comradeship that will linger
even as we pass on to the better place.

A particular shout out to Crazy Jack Waer
and his evil tempered pet monkey Chuck..
I swear, Jack, some nights when the wind is right,
I still hear the sound from across the Mohave Desert
way off there in your treasured mountains of Arizona,
you tap, tap, tapping out your TANS stories
of high dangers met with courage and spirit.

And to you, Mad Denny;
you somehow defeated all the odds
and fought your own way back.

And, most important, to Lynnie
Who has helped me from those times to these..
To you, my true princess, a special love salute.
I'm sure there has to be such a tender gesture
in a place somewhere specially preserved
for those who do their very best
to love and guide the Old Spooks & Spies.

CONTENTS

ACKNOWLEDGMENTS

A few years ago, when I heard Paul Kengor had written a book detailing 'how America's adversaries have manipulated Progressives for a Century', I had to buy a copy to see for myself how anyone could risk a career by making such an outlandish claim.

From the first, I found DUPES interesting historical reading. The Russian leaders – Marx, Lenin, Stalin, Brezhnev – were well known figures, as were left leaning Hollywood personalities and New York literary types..

But on page 283 history came real for me; there Kengor mentions a man named Gus Hall as the general secretary of the CPUSA starting in 1959. Back then, I didn't even know there was a functioning Communist Party of the United States of America, much less that in 1966 it would firm up plans to enlist leftist Western intellectuals in a propaganda campaign to undermine U.S. forces in Vietnam. But I did know Gus Hall. He tried to recruit me on the UCLA campus in 1962.

Today it is a part of the progressive litany – you hear it from educators and fifth columnists alike – that the anti-Vietnam Movement in the U.S. started spontaneously around 1965 as some sort of humanistic ground swell reaction to overseas U.S. aggression. But I knew differently. I had attended a rally at UCLA in 1962 where I was asked to hand out pamphlets with a crude sketch on the front of a U.S. tank about to crush some startled peasants wearing cone hats. Stop The U.S. Invader Gangster Colonialists! the headline screamed.

Several years later, as a member of U.S. Military Intelligence with a Top Secret clearance, I would translate the same words from covert Viet Cong messages, De Quoc Xam Luoc My. *Invader Gangster Americans.*

You have to give the CPUSA, the Viet Minh, the Viet Cong and communists everywhere credit for a political movement tenaciously applied that encouraged American youth to flag stomping, protest marches, draft card burnings, and throwing pigs blood, as well as fleeing to Canada and Sweden…a propaganda campaign that eventually brought down the war.

That was the history, but with a relevance for today. Believe it or not, nations and groups that continue to dislike the U.S. currently are still trying to pull us down. Different slogans, but the same goal.

Some despair that America is lost. I personally do not think that is true. As my Midwestern pioneer ancestors advised, *You know there's still meat on the table so long as the wild dogs are howling around outside.*

JOHN KLAWITTER

HICKORY NUTS

September, 1949. See the young girl dancing seventy feet in the air at the top of a giant hickory tree while her kid brother clings to a thick branch further down. The tree is in the middle of a broad flatland meadow, all oak browns, maple reds and the dry grass look of a late Indian summer. It is the third year, the bumper crop year, and the branches are heavy with hickory nuts wrapped in their leathery green husks

Looking up into the great tree, Lucy Rose's lips whisper *Hail Mary full of grace* as she tries to keep at least the outward appearance of her normally calm and placid self. But how can she with her two young children swaying up there where every moment, every next move could send them crashing to the hard ground?

"This is a bad idea, Bill. Somebody is going to fall!" she says.

"Well, it won't be Jack junior," Bill scoffs. Flinty humor shows on his weather-lined face. Grown brother and sister, Bill and Lu have their hands folded over their heads as they dodge intermittent spatters of leathery green nuts. "You and I were climbing trees practically before we could walk."

"Well, it was different in our time." Lucy gasps as way up there young Mary boldly flings herself like a woods sprite from one branch to another as if gravity doesn't exist, no possible way the lithe and graceful girl could fall. A fresh shower of nuts pelts down around them, hitting the ground like big green hailstones.

Bill, the son and grandson and great grandson of local farmers, knows where the interesting wildlife still grows in the forest preserves, not only the hickory and walnuts, but the elderberries, raspberries and wild grapes, the small sweet wild strawberries, and still other plants gone wild: asparagus and endive and cherries and even the lone apple tree Granddaddy Michael swore was planted by Johnny Appleseed himself.

Lucy and Bill started their lives on the family farm, homesteaded a hundred years before on lands freshly vacated by the Sauk and Fox Indian tribes. Free to roam over hundreds of acres of fields and meadows, Lucy had been climbing trees practically before she started grade school. Her eldest, Mary, now dancing way up there in the thin treetop branches, is nearly a teenager. Jack, Jr., a year and a half younger, is barely ten feet overhead, clinging desperately with both arms wrapped around a thick branch. He was baptized John, like his dad, but his dad is commonly called Jack, and so he is Jack, Jr. to some and John, Johnny, Johnny-boy to others.

"Fraidy cat! Fraidy cat!" Mary yells down at him. "Johnny is a fraidy cat!"

He stubbornly shakes his head. "Somebody has to shake off the ones down here," he yells back at her.

Bill shouts encouragement, though Lu's kid is only ten feet overhead. Bill is a little hard of hearing, and maybe it is the excitement of the moment.

"Johnny, the way to do it is, you get a firm hold with one hand, then reach out and get a firm hold with the other one before you let go your first handhold."

"Ha, ha, ha," the voice from on high floats down to them, "There are no nuts down there except you, little brother!"

Jack, Jr.'s face takes on a set look of concentration and he carefully lets go with one hand, snaking it out to take a death grip on a nearby branch. Then he repeats the gesture with the other hand, awkwardly shuttling out toward the edge of the tree where a few nuts hang.

Lucy shakes her head, "He just doesn't seem to have a knack for it."

Bill shrugs it off. As a slight and bandy-legged youth, he himself had been underestimated if not outright dismissed.

"He may not climb high, Lu, but he listens sharp and he gets the idea real fast. And you see he doesn't let go."

It is an interesting moment in forecasting the children's futures. Mary, who will break her mother's heart a dozen times, will in the coming decades give a fortune away to prophets, wise men and grifters who ply the spirituality game. She will sit at the feet of the great masters of East Indian philosophy and have a narrow turn with one particularly nasty white-robed cult master in Oregon, and will somehow always find ways to save herself just before she comes plummeting down to earthly disaster. And Jack, Jr., once he has an idea in hand and a plan of action, will cling to his path with a fierce tenacity beyond notions popular or fashionable for his place and time, that is the latter half of the twentieth century and the first decade of the twenty-first. Whether in this he showed admirable perseverance, or delusion bordering on madness, you who live in your own time may decide for yourselves.

HUMMINGBIRD ON THE FORTY-THIRD

Late-summer, 1989. At this time, Jack is an absent minded fifty-year-old moonlight writer who makes a decent daytime living directing semi-brainless television commercials for breakfast cereals and underarm deodorants. He owns an army footlocker half-full of unsold novel manuscripts that he stores in his garage in the San Fernando Valley. In the first few years after he came back from his war he furiously scribbled anything that came to mind on any scrap of paper at hand, but as the rejection letters piled up he slowed down and took a second look, and then a third. He got smarter, shaved off the poetry and the self-conscious nonsense, learned pacing and started to figure out how to tell a story. And now when it was almost too late, somebody had finally nibbled at the bait.

He was walking past Macy's in New York City, the one where they'd filmed *Miracle on 34th Street*. It being the wrong season for sleigh bells and jolly fat men, Macy's looked about like any other department store. He frowned at his reflection in a plate glass window. He saw a somewhat frayed fellow who still ran 10Ks to stay in shape, now graying around the edges and sagging a little in the middle. He felt hollow and uncertain; the commercial *director* inside, that part of him that barked *Action!* and *Cut!* and *Okay people, let's do another one!* was nowhere to be found, at least not for the moment.

He floated along in the dreamlike state he drifted into when he was alone for any length of time. He was not like this when he was in the flow and chatter of film or vid production or the hasty grin, grab and *see ya later* of a wrap party. In those hustling and triumphant moments he had none of these empty, sad feelings. He caught himself looking at his reflection in the Macy's window and at the same time he was thinking about looking in the window, he was also thinking about writing about looking in the window.

He wondered when this sick habit of pulling back from the moment had actually begun. He hadn't been this way in the shallow monotony of his uneventful youth trapped in an industrial Midwestern town. Something had happened to him in 1964 or '65. Was it that innocence-withering moment on Tu Do Street when the wide-eyed young terrorist pointed an ancient revolver at him and blew off three shots in his direction from point blank range? Or was it a grisly visual image of a little kid's small, neatly amputated foot with the white cotton stocking and the light blue tennis shoe still on it lying on the sidewalk a half-block away from where a car bomb went off outside the U.S. Embassy? Was it the intestines hanging like prankster's toilet paper from a tree outside the shattered Brinks Bachelor Officers Quarters? All of these, and more, he thought, though there was no way for him to really know if those old images were still affecting him in any way that mattered, and he certainly wasn't going to see a shrink about any of that. He had ridden his luck through a bit of a chain saw movie and nothing from those times back there could touch him. He was here on the other side now, and that bad business was in the long ago and far away.

He stared at the ghost of himself in the glass. In the little room behind his reflection real manikins in chic autumn outfits played out a scene with pumpkins and dried corn stalks, telling him summer was played out, winter coming on. A taxi rippled by in the reflection. He turned to call it, but naturally, he was too late. The muggy August heat beat on his bare head. He should have worn one of his panama straw hats, all the rage in Hollywood. He trudged on, taking his steps one by one, the way he always did.

He was standing on a shiny marble floor in the lobby of a big skyscraper in the publishing district, wondering if he really wanted to go through with this. He was back in his dreamlike state. He was the hero in the story about going to see his new editor, and he was at his typewriter, writing the story. He looked wondering and witless, younger than he actually was.

He was remembering Sergeant Moore's ruined face with the chunks torn out of it and the drugged look as his crossed eyes peered up at him from a bed in Saigon General, and he wondered if there was such a thing as a functioning PTSD. He caught his reflection in the mirrored aluminum face of the elevator. The proof was in the pudding; not a scratch on him. But that was silly; that was so many years back down the road behind him, how could any of that matter now? The doors parted and he stepped in and was on his way up.

His appointment was on the 43rd floor. The elevator dumped him off at 30. He had to walk in a little semi-circle to another brushed metal door that silently opened to invite him the rest of the way. A pair of young secretaries eyed him and then silently moved to the opposite corner of the little aluminum box. A few more moments of swift rising and he was in a glossy waiting room, a reception area with low leather chairs and one wall entirely floor-to-ceiling glass, a dramatic view looking out and down on the sheer vertical walls and cliffs of the Manhattan skyline.

An odd flash of color caught his eye. There was a little thing outside, a hovering, darting jewel that gave off flashes of citrine, emerald and reddish-gold in the sooty city sunlight. Beale saw it was attracted to the lavender and cream petals of a giant potted orchid on his side of the glass. He would not have believed it could fly so high.

The receptionist pointed to the tan leather chairs.

"Mr. Wister is running late." She sounded like it happened a lot.

It was a bad chair, built for show, and he had to work at not slumping down into the seat. A lean, literary type slouched in one of the chairs down the line from him dismissed him with a flickering glance.

Jack eyed the fellow. He was maybe forty, and was wearing rubber-treaded hiking boots, khaki pants, a tan shirt and a photographer's vest with dozens of pockets. *The war reporter look,* he thought. A clothing outfit that said I'm just back from the Middle East. Just in from the

Killing Fields of Cambodia. Just turned in my story on the genocide horrors in North Africa. *Was that what authors were wearing these days?* The guy had a pocket full of pens and a straight patrician nose fronted with small, round, wire-rimmed John Lennon glasses. The savvy intellectual look. That is how Jack would have cast the guy if he was an actor selected to do a commercial for some deodorant preferred by intellectual men of action and adventure: *Lucky Boy Gel - takes the edge off the smell of fear!*

What was he doing in this posh and quiet lobby in the heart of the publishing district in Manhattan? Jack's spirit sagged. Life wasn't fair, but here it was again, the pick of the bad straw staring him in the face. He'd simply gone for the wrong war, or as he'd been told, *it had picked him.*

He had tapped key after endless key with a dogged single-mindedness, churning out the stories of his lessons learned in his war, the bad war, the wrong war. He had burnished his skills at writing query letters. He was sure his work was better, truer, and more vital now than it had been in the heat of the moment. What the hell was so wrong about him being here? *Something. Something crazy. Stupid.* The chuckling ghost of Hemingway, sipping scotch as he glances from his typewriter out across the warm Caribbean water north of Havana, *It's not like plucking apples from the tree, you know.*

Jack wanted to be like this other guy; bright, optimistic, aggressive, a rising star, a writer on his way up. But his attention snagged on the purple sprig of drying flowers in his lapel, and he could see now that stopping in D.C. was a mistake. He'd snapped it off a wilting wreath somebody had laid next to the names etched on the wall, his small token to take back to the West Coast, something to say *Yeah, I was there. Yeah, I still remember all of you.*

But, no. He was here now and everything was wrong, wrong, wrong. He was sweating, overheated from his walk along the Manhattan streets. He should have been a little quicker; he should have caught that taxi. Damp was staining the thin shirt under his California chic black-and-white checked sport coat, panic coming on strong now. Damn. He should have worn an undershirt. His soft leather Bally boots were wrong too, somehow so 1970's. Why was this expensive Sy Devore outfit that was so right when he was directing on the set so out of place here? No two ways about it. His damn miserable stupid jacket was too loud, too West Coast, out of place and out of time. His fingers fumbled at his red-and-yellow striped tie.

The lean, literary type eyed him with bemused disinterest. *Get with it,* his attitude said. *In another few months it will be 1990. Nobody gives a crap about your stupid old war any more, if they ever did.* Jack shifted his weight, ready to get to his feet and bolt for the elevator, but the timing was against him as the elevator doors opened and a look-alike to the first literary type ambled into the waiting room. This second author also was lean and angular. He wore the same round, wire-rimmed glasses and similar clunky hiking boots. But he wasn't a carbon copy; the checkered arms of his Pendleton shirt indicated he was a woodsman and a nature buff. The newcomer sighed, stretched and nodded to the photographer type.

"Edward. How's your muse treating you?

"Greedy, rotten bitch. How's about you, Martin?"

"Turning in my pages."

"Been waiting long?"

"Nah, maybe ten minutes. Wister's running late."

Locke Wister, Jack's contact. Jack frowned and studied his highly polished boots. He placed his stiff sided Samsonite briefcase on his lap, clicked it open and took out a book he'd bought earlier that day at a small shop on Lexington Avenue. The bookseller was an odd old man with a full white beard. A wrinkled oldster with a white plastic construction hat on his head with the big letters CPC stenciled on the front. Between the hat sitting down to his bushy white eyebrows and the beard pushing up to his nose, his peering black eyes were two peas in a bowl of chowder.

"Why are you wearing that hat?" Jack had asked the old man.

"So nothing falls on my head."

"What does CPC stand for?"

"Canoga Power Company. You want the book?"

"How much is it?"

"Fifty dollars."

"That's a lot for a used book."

"Fifty dollars," the invisible mouth under the droopy white moustache repeated.

It was a heavy rectangle in his hands, A Little Tour of France, by American Henry James, that polished scribbler from the lost times and trials of the Victorian era. The opening pages noted Mr. James had hurriedly handwritten batches of notes, apologized for their hasty accumulation, and hoped to have them published with some black-and-white sketches of cottages and cathedrals to be done by a man named Joseph Pennell. The sketches had not been forthcoming in a timely manner, so the words were published alone in 1884, and then with the sketches in a separate edition in 1900. The book Jack held in his hands was a recent edition, printed in 1988 and it included not only the sketches, but also color plates by French impressionists as well as color maps tracing the early routes Mr. James had taken.

As he browsed through the pages, Jack was struck by an at-first-glance seemingly odd similarity between the lives of the rural French citizens in that golden time before the two World Wars and the simplicity of the peasant way of life in the hamlet society of South Vietnam before mortar rounds started looping in from the East and West on those trying to farm the rice paddies in the middle.

Jack's imagination left the waiting room in the air high above the ant-busy streets of Manhattan. He daydreamed he was back in the late 1890s and he was walking beside a pretty French girl past thatched roof houses on a path along a row of birch trees beside a pleasant brook. And then he was walking with a comely bargirl on her day off from the Cherry Bar and it was back before the Nam war really started up in earnest. And then back in France again, only twenty years later, and he wondered that those simple peasants had somehow been transmogrified into companies of soup plate helmeted troopers with rifles and strange alien looking gas masks. And that led him to wonder how poor simple peasant rice farmers living in isolated bamboo villages could be convinced to spend their spare time manufacturing homemade Bouncing

Bettys and aiming AK47s that were made half a world away in Czechoslovakia. You don't fight tanks with bamboo rakes and water buffalos. His mind spun idly for a time, putting down the possibility that his half-formed and disconnected thoughts could lead to anything rational or even useful.

After a time he did doze off and he flew away into a dream where two dark clouds were squabbling over the best way to grow a lotus flower from a single patch of fertile soil, and in his drowsy state he thought he might be on to something, but then his dream was interrupted by surface chatter in the here and now and he came back with a start to the lobby in Manhattan.

"This guy is wearing a 'Nam Vet's pin," Martin the maybe hiker-scribbler said.

Jack started awake. The fellow was talking about him. He slid A Little Tour in France back in his briefcase and placed it on the floor between his legs. He was thinking *Hey, I'm right here and you're talking about me as if I am nothing and nobody.* But he didn't say anything. Maybe he should have, but he didn't.

"And a tie made out of the South Vietnamese flag," Edward the perhaps conflict reporter added.

"Semophoric attire."

"He could have tried the Viet Cong flag. More colorful."

Jack frowned. "You know the flags, but you didn't go?"

The photographer type grinned and trumpeted like Frankenstein's creator, "It's alive!" But after a moment of silence, he more seriously considered Jack's simple question, "Nobody went except *the stupids*. Nobody *had* to go."

"You don't remember John F. Kennedy, the President of the United States, asking patriot soldiers to help fight brushfire wars?"

"Kennedy was a Democrat, you ass. Republicans start wars."

"Back in 1961 JFK called on us to beat back the communists."

"Yeah, yeah, right. Something about countries toppling like Monopoly pieces. He sure got that one wrong."

The hiker type chanted wearily, *"LBJ, LBJ, how many kids did you kill today?"*

Jack felt his blood rising. "Like *dominos*! And they all fell, except Thailand!"

Before he could say anything more, the elevator doors opened and two fat middle-aged Jewish men in drag hopped out and flounced through the lobby and into the reception area like a dance number out of a way, way off-Broadway musical. Their dark chins showed two days of stubble, their cheeks were rouged, their heavy red lipstick was a crimson mess, they were chewing dead cigars, and their nylons were rolled half way down their hairy, stocky calves. Their slips stuck out an inch or so below their knee-high skirts and big padded bras projected from their chests like the prows of twin gunboats. They wore tennis shoes, they didn't care a hoot their big fat feet could never fit in high heels.

They approached the reception desk with a mincing dance step, lustily singing the opening to the Bugs Bunny cartoon show. The receptionist brightened when she saw them and they were ushered into the inner sanctum, still singing "Ta-Da-duh-da-da-dut-dut-da!"

"So you didn't go?" Jack's question dropped like a pebble into the silence that followed. "Neither of you went?"

"You still talking about that?" Martin the nature loving hiker type asked. "Look, Dumb-As-A-Brick Wonder-Boy, we didn't have to go. None of us. Bad eyes. Nerve disease. Mental what-the-fuck aversion. You got a slip from the doc. If you were in too good a shape, he could always inject water in your knees." He grinned knowingly at Jack, "At least that's what got me out." The happy recollection faded from his face, "Screwed up my knees ever since, though."

"But that only meant somebody else had to go in your place."

"Better him than me." Martin turned to Edward the maybe photographer. "You notice how gays are the big banana these days?"

"The Wister has a nose for the new thing. I don't know how he does it."

"Editors don't edit anymore," Martin snorted. "They are advertising men, sell-out *literary marketeers*."

Edward nodded his agreement. "You don't even want to show up around here without a pre-edit. That's *our* responsibility anymore."

"Not fair. We pay big bucks for some schmuck to do what's supposed to be Wister's job."

The lingering scent of heavy perfume hung in the air. Edward wrinkled his nose, "Imitation queers piss me off."

"Don't they know their cover is blown?"

"They don't care. How long has *La Cage aux Folles* been at the West End?"

"I tell you, our pal Mister Wister is never wrong – They come dancing in here, *faux light loafers* are the coming thing."

"I don't get why butt sex is such a big deal. Christ, anybody could be gay."

"Maybe you should try it."

"Speak for yourself."

"Money to be made. Think of the titles: Being Queer. Gay Today. The Flip Side. The Crowded Closet."

"Man's got a dick; I guess it doesn't matter where you stick it."

"The coming thing, I tell you."

The elevator doors opened to cast out a gaunt thirty-ish girl dressed in ankle-length black chiffon that swirled like Pigpen's dirt as she walked. She wore white powder facial makeup and black rings around her eyes. Her nails were purple and a large golden ring pierced one corner of her lip.

"Goth," Martin the hiker whispered, rolling his eyes with a shake of his head.

Jack had a vision of Henry James and Hemingway sitting on wicker chairs on the outdoor patio of a French Café in the countryside. No matter that it is just outside of Da Nang and not near Le Mans, the air has the sweet tang of spring and the late afternoon light shines with the soft amber glow of Keats-ian poetry and the tired peasants are making their contented way home from the fields to a nearby hamlet village. Henry is drinking pommeau from a lacquered Thanh Le cup and Ernest raises a glass of green absinthe *parisienne* and they both smile as if toasting an old friend. Henry's cup is carved with the ancient *Tu Do Mot* design of the monkey teasing an old man while an evil goat looks on. The message is clear. Jack stands and picks up his briefcase.

Henry and Ernest are gone, but not a moment ago they were out there, just on the other side of the glass near where the flashing jewel of a hummingbird had floated on the air. Jack steadily marches for the elevator, one foot in front of the other.

"Tell Mr. Wister I had another appointment." He speaks loud enough so the literary types can overhear him.

The receptionist places a blush pink finger nail on her pulp romance novel and looks up at him.

"Wooh!" Edward, the would-be war correspondent slings a pseudo *sotto voce* across the room.

"Wooh, wooh, wooh!" Martin is happy. "I guess we move up the line."

The Goth girl says nothing, giving off a blank glare intended for life in general as if, to her, the people in the room have no significance.

Jack waits for the elevator door to open. The little bird is gone, or maybe he'd just imagined it in the first place. A woman who reminds him of his high school drama teacher is standing next to him, impatient for the doors to open, the stack of manuscripts heavy in her arms. She notices he is looking at the big orchid plant.

"They aren't real, you know." She dismisses the waxy dark green leaves and shoots of exotic flowers with a nod of her gray-streaked curls. "Marvelous imitations, though, don't you think?"

HOW HE PLAYED THE GAME

October 1949   Where was he? Where was he? Where was he? Jack, Jr's mind raced in circles, going nowhere. *No matter where, he was drowning. He surfaced into* a bleary sort of consciousness to find himself clinging to the memory of his cherry tree, an odd thing, maybe, for an eleven-year-old kid to be so desperate for something like that. His precious tree had been split in half by lightning two years before. His dad had wanted to cut it down, but Jack, Jr. threw one of the few major fits of his youth, and though the poor refugee from an orchard ended up looking strange and off-balance, they had yielded to his childish rage and pruned one side back to the split in the stump and kept the rest.

He was in his bed, in his home, in Steger, the town the great piano maker had built by stoking the dreams of *tishlers* from Europe. His body ached and he felt punk-miserable all over. His bones, his joints, even the blood in his veins burned. When other kids got sick with chicken pox or the measles, they suffered a miserable few days and shrugged it off. Jack, Jr. was different. His high fevers were a family legend; one he survived on the farm when he was three or four had left him near-sighted and (his sister claimed) half-witted, though under questioning she confessed to anyone who would listen he may have been that before.

This new sickness, the one that had him thinking of angels and cherry trees, was different; it had him gasping for air, unable to catch a breath, his lungs full of phlegm. His fever spiked at 105 and stayed there until his mom lowered him naked into a bath tub filled with icy water. After that the fever subsided, but his stomach churned and he was seasick. A hatchet chopped deep into his skull with regularly timed blows. He was going to die. He *wanted* to die.

But he lingered while some remote awareness had him thinking of his cherry tree, out there in the back yard. After that summer storm and the bolt of lightning, it had never been the same. And yet every spring a gift of sweet black cherries would hang from the branches.

After the five day attack his fierce illness left him savaged and strangely altered; the left side of his face remained normal while the right was numb, frozen as if it had turned to warm stone. He couldn't feel his fingers touching the skin, couldn't blink or shut his eye, couldn't smile. He drooled and his dragging lips slurred his speech.

"Bell's palsy," Doctor McDonnell declared. He shook his head as he put his stethoscope back in his carrying case, the diagnosis the end of his responsibility. The portly doctor brushed cigarette ashes from his wrinkled black suit vest and stood, ready to turn toward the door and his next house call.

"How can we pay you?" Jack, Jr.'s mother asked.

The doctor smiled sadly, understanding the question.

"Pay me when you can," he said.

"W-when will I get better?" Jack, Jr. called from the bed.

"Your mom needs to buy you an eye patch from Walgreens, so you can sleep at night."

"But – "

"It's a form of polio, Jack, Jr.," the doctor said, his voice raising a notch. "There is no cure for it."

"But – "

"You're one of the lucky ones, son. There are kids like you crippled for life, on crutches, or worse; boys and girls your age trapped inside iron lungs."

"No cure for it," Jack, Jr. whispered. He confided in no one, but in his secret place in his mind, he recognized this was entirely his fault. He'd been giddy with victory, gotten too far out on the limb, forgotten it was one hand safely in front of the other.

He softly slurred the words. "That will never happen again."

The Steger VFW junior softball team was something of a joke around town, as much as the sad village joked about anything since stunned by the Great Depression and the disappearance of the piano company pension fund. Folks knew the VFW Blues were just a scrape-together, a pain-in-the-butt last minute add-on because there were too many kids left over after the real teams were picked. The left-overs were given dark blue shirts with VFW hurriedly sewn on the back by an old Italian lady from the dry cleaners.

The Veterans of Foreign Wars was a small liquor bar that, in principle, catered only to men who had served overseas in World War II, with a sprinkling of old geezers from that earlier war that had proposed to end all wars. The owner of the bar was a relatively prosperous and jovial fellow who agreed to pick up the tab for the Blues. There was no time or money to add individual player numbers, but what did it matter, anyway? It was a good cause, something to keep the kids out of trouble for the summer.

Jack, Jr. would rather have settled in with one of the John Carter Mars books from his uncle, but his dad had been a pitcher with the Steger *Hoitemts* back in the day, and when Jack, Jr. saw Jack, Sr. wanted it, he put on a show of enthusiasm. Problem was, Jack, Jr. was in long-term denial over his nearsightedness, and he was squinting around without glasses. He saw the ball well enough to take wild swings at it, the grounders tended to blacken his eyes and bloody his nose, and he threw like a refugee from spastics anonymous. So for him VFW Blue was a loser deal from the get-go. On a team of bad players he was clearly the worst; other teams routinely hit the ball to him, assuring that their worst batters would safely get on base.

Jack, Sr. came to see one game, but there wasn't anything to cheer about, so after a few innings he saw his son hadn't picked up the game by genetic osmosis. He left early and stopped in at the VFW. He hadn't been in any foreign wars or even in the army, but everybody in town knew they made exceptions. And, after all, he would have gone if they had asked him.

As the season wore on, the Blues built an uninterrupted losing record. Discouraged players dropped out until the frustrated coach had to stick Jack, Jr. out behind second base all the time, and nobody was happy.

There was an autumn chill in the air as the season finally wore down to the last game. Jack, Jr. wasn't feeling anything but relief as he stubbornly trudged out to his position, the spot behind second base where the rest of the infield players could shade over and try to cover his mistakes.

The first batter slapped a sharp grounder in his direction, but by some miracle the ball stuck to his glove and he flipped to first base for an easy out. The Steger Drug Store Reds held an emergency meeting behind home plate and made the fatal mistake of changing their strategy. They figured they must have heard something wrong; this guy was actually pretty good. From then on they slapped the ball here and there, feeling for weaknesses. But, miracle of miracles, on that day the Blues showed no holes in the dike, no fumbles, no errant throws. Even Jack, Jr. survived his second chance, catching an easy pop fly for an out.

Scoring runs was another matter, but in the last inning the frustrated Reds pitcher walked in a run, and the Blues took the game, one to nothing. There was such jubilation in the single low bench that passed for bleachers you would have thought the Blues had won the World Series.

Cheery Howie, the owner of the VFW, invited the entire team over to the bar on Dixie Highway for Cokes and potato chips on the house, and Elmer the police chief grinned and said that would be alright, he would look the other way as this was a monumental occasion.

Jack, Jr. hadn't actually gotten a hit, but his walk had brought in the winning run and he was flushed with the thrill of a victory that was undeniably partly of his own doing. He hopped on his battered Schwinn and raced along with his teammates to pick up their chips and drinks. The night was turning cold, but they were sweating by the time they skidded into the parking lot behind the bar. Inside, the darkened room was lit with neon Blatz signs and a back lit picture of a mechanical waterfall. The warm air had a beery smell, and the Blues practically gobbled up their bags of chips and washed them down with their big Cokes.

The party was over practically before it started. In a flash, the team gave a last cheer and disbanded in the parking lot. Jack, Jr. pedaled furiously for home to pass on the tremendous news. But his dad had choir practice, which meant he would spend time after that lingering over a Schlitz or two at the Orchard Tavern. And Lucy Rose had his brother Tommy and his sisters Barbara and Zan down on their knees, half way through a rosary. You didn't interrupt a rosary with kid's chatter about a softball game. Jack, Jr. reached for the rosary by his place at the table and got down on his knees. His shirt and pants were damp with perspiration and he was starting to feel shivery, but they only had two more strings of ten Hail Marys to go. The really bad first wave of his sickness didn't set in for another few hours, by then the middle of the night. The family worked hard just to keep food on the table and he wasn't going to wake anybody up.

Once he showed up for class at St. Liborius wearing his black eye patch, he was a heroic figure for about a week before the banter started. *Some pirate, man! Where's your sword? We're playing Batman, how's about you get to be the Joker?*

Sitting behind her big oak desk in the front of the nearly empty classroom, stern little Sister Cresentia watched Jack screw up his face, over and over and over again. He was trying to hide behind his Reading Book, but that wasn't working at all for him. The diminutive nun couldn't decide if he was just crazy or if the devil had taken over his mind. Finally, she stormed down the aisle with a heavy ruler in her good right hand. "Jack Beale, stop fooling around! What are you doing?"

"Exercising my face, Sister."

"You look horrible! Awful! Stop it right now! Did the doctor tell you to do that?"

"No. He said it was useless."

"Then I am telling you to stop right now! You'll frighten the other children!"

Jack, Jr. stared at her while he continued to squinch his face like a prune and then let it relax, over and over again. The nun raised the thick wooden ruler in her hand, ready to beat some serious common sense in him, but even that didn't make him stop.

Instead, he slowly stood to face her. The sister was a short person, barely reaching five feet in her black shoes with the one inch lifts, and in that moment Jack, Jr. was at the same level as she was.

"You'll have to kill me," he said quietly.

Stunned at this threat to her authority, the nun quickly looked around to make sure they were alone in the room. She breathed a sigh of relief. No one had seen or heard the craziness that was taking place.

"Okay. Okay," she hissed. "But never, ever when another student can see you."

He nodded and sank back into his seat. He continued his facial exercises. He was some sort of dervish going through an odd, never ending ritual. She blessed herself with the sign of the cross and turned the other way so she wouldn't have to look at him.

It was eight months before Jack, Jr. could open and close his right eye, and it took him several years to regain some of the control over his mouth and cheeks and other facial muscles. By then, his exercises were a habit he would keep for the rest of his life.

"I have never seen anything like that before," Doctor McDonnell said. "I think your boy is controlling the paralyzed muscles on that side of his face from the other side. Not supposed to happen. Something of a marvel, in my opinion." The doctor briefly thought about doing a paper on it, but then he realized he was too busy to get into something like that. Fooling around with a scientific paper would just be a waste of time; the medical magazines didn't really consider articles by unknown rural practitioners.

Three years later, a big wind storm snapped off the remaining half of Jack, Jr.'s cherry tree. After that, his mother told him there was nothing left to rescue and they would just have to saw off the trunk for firewood and dig out the roots. He wasn't upset by the loss. The tree had been there when he needed it.

THE MOON AIR BOYS

October 1989.   The cops are calling Frankie a scum-
bag – off the record, of course, because the investigation
is still pending and they haven't caught the guys who did
him in. They know Frankie was renting a warehouse
where they found a lot of Thai stick and a few bales of
dope worth a couple million dollars on the street. Sure, it's
an open-and-shut case, but none of that matters, because
Frankie's gone forever, and no matter what the
investigators find out or the papers say, I know who really
killed him. It was me, his best buddy.

We were old pals; we went a long way back. And
what we had most in common was that we never grew out
of our crazy, youthful dreams, even though we both were
pushing fifty when the hit came down on Frankie. We'd
get together and our wives would just shake their heads
because we wouldn't talk about our regular jobs or
bricking in the patio, we'd be arguing about writing novels
or planning a movie or trying to figure out the best way to
get down to Tierra del Fuego to look for diamonds.

At least it went fast for Frankie. A young black guy pushed past his startled receptionist and stood in the middle of his big mortgage broker suite, which was in a good location near downtown Portland.

"Mister Wilson! Hey, Wilson! Where are you, my man?!" the black kid yelled.

"There's no Mr. Wilson here," Frankie said. He'd come out of his private office to see what the fuss was all about. He should have known – a leather-jacketed black kid wearing a baseball cap with a Porsche crest on it wasn't there to buy a house. Maybe he did know, but before he could do anything, the punk took a pistol from his pocket and shot a hole in his chest. Then he leaned over and carefully blew away the back of his head. He executed Frankie in broad daylight, the middle of the work day with phones jangling and loans being approved, the splattered red giving the poor secretaries a taste of life in the dark woods where the sheep never go.

The kid calmly stuck his gun in his pocket and pushed his way through the onlookers, who were starting to mill and scream. He was picked up outside by a buddy in a get-away car, just like the movies, except it was Frankie – my Frankie – still shuddering as his flesh cooled and his blood seeped into the beige carpet.

He was a feisty Italian kid from Bayonne who enjoyed art movies and good food, and I was a farm-boy from Illinois with a couple of college degrees and a lot of hayseed in my hair. He'd worked as hard as I had to get through college, and he had an annoying way of popping my balloons. We met at Army Language School in Monterey, argued a lot about Camus and Sartre, football and boxing, woman and women, and he claimed I saved his life in Vietnam.

I didn't, really. It was sort of a scam. It was early in 1965, and I was working for the 3rd Radio Research Unit at Tan Son Nhut, the big air base just west of Saigon. I'd been translating covert Viet Cong messages almost a year when Frankie shipped in-country. He'd been stationed in the Philippines where they did the same thing to off-shore electronics picked up by our destroyers like the Turner Joy, which you may remember was involved in the phony "Hai Phong Incident" that fooled congress into passing the Tonkin Resolution to give the 'Nam War, for a time, a certain tarnished sense of legality.

Anyway, Frankie called, his voice sounding frightened and tinny on the antiquated French phone system, and he used my nickname from language school, "Kha, I'm in big trouble!"

"Frankie! What's the problemo, Mister Romance? Pineapple Girls give you a dose of the big C?"

"Can the jokes, Kha! I been loaned to the 3rd, and they're shipping me into the bush!"

"Not to worry, Hondo; I've been there. You just camp out, sort of, and listen to the static through your headphones 'til fungus grows in your ears. Six weeks later you come back, we lay a few girls at the Chez Rene and -"

"No, no, no, NO! I'm not going to die out there! I had a bad dream about this! And you gotta help!"

"Me?! I'm a lowly Spec.5, Frankie!"

"Kha, you got to! That's what friends do!"

To this day I don't know why, but I shrugged into my

tropical tans, took off my name tag and borrowed a Jeep from the motor pool. By the time I negotiated a few potholed side-streets and drove across the sticky-hot tarmac, Frankie's outfit was settling into a big, semi-permanent tent-barracks. I strode in like one of the mean, power-tripping son-of-a-bitches you see everywhere in the military.

"Magonia! Where the goddam holy hell's Spec. 4 Magonia!?"

No officers were around and my lowly bar-over-eagle ranked everybody in the place.

A wide-eyed corporal actually saluted me. "Ah - over there, sir!" he said, while the rest of them kept their noses in their shoe polish.

Frankie came, dragging his duffel bag.

I barked, "They want you over at the 3rd!" And stalked out of there before anyone could get a good look at me. Once we were out of sight I swung the jeep around and headed for the main gate. He borrowed a few thousand piasters and the last I saw; he was heaving his bag into the back seat of a blue-and-cream *xe hoi* taxi.

He shacked up with a doe-eyed girl he met at the Cherry Bar and spent the next few weeks dining with the officers at the haut French Tour D'Argent, Le Bistro, Chez Brodard cafe, the Hai Cua crab house, and Cheap Charley's Chinese where the food was served American-style with knives and forks on white linen. He actually showed up at the 3rd RRU every week or so to read the bulletin board in front of our C.O.'s office, and to jaw with some of the lingies he knew from Monterey while he stood in the pay line. They paid him, too, and it was eight weeks before anybody caught on that he wasn't assigned duty or even living on the base.

It finally did hit the fan, and the C.O. furiously pushed for a court martial, but Frankie managed to have the legalities shifted back to the Philippines where he pleaded it was just another army screw up. He always could talk his way out of anything, right until the end.

A few years later, I was back in Chicago writing Kellogg's Corn Flakes spots for the Captain Kangaroo Show when Frankie showed up in town for a pharmaceutical convention. We stood on the bridge where Michigan Avenue crosses over the Chicago River, looking at the white castle-like Wrigley Building, laughing over old times and dropping peanut shells in the oil-slicked water, below. He'd married Billie, a girl he'd met in Monterey before 'Nam, and he was working in New York City for one of the big drug companies.

"I handle a chunk of Manhattan," he said in his typical bemused way. "My job is, I drop off free samples of birth control pills to the saw-bones. 'Course, lots of the samples gets liberated." He beamed happily. "Like we was liberating the free peoples of 'Nam."

"Isn't that - dangerous?"

"Naaa. All the reps do it. Only way to make a living, Kha." He laughed his great laugh and I didn't think any more about it. He said he was moving to Oregon so they could be near Billie's dad, who had a bad heart. We went to the Stockyards Inn and chewed over some great Mid-West steaks, Coleridge and Pantheism, the New York Giants and the Bears, and the Tom Kelly photo of Marilyn Monroe naked pink on red velvet as a universal symbol of perfection.

I won an EMMY for a documentary I did on the death of Robert Kennedy and got married and moved to Hollywood. Frankie was best man at my wedding, godfather to my son. By this time, he'd given up on the pill game and was working at a mortgage company, and pretty soon, he went out on his own. Meanwhile, I was taking whatever scraps I could get – commercials, cable shows, and industrials – from the underbelly of show business.

Frankie had offered a dozen times to get me a re-fi home loan, and I finally called him after a client who owed me 50 grand unexpectedly left for Ixtapa-Zihuatanejo.

"Even you can't pull this one off," I said. "My income isn't high enough."

Frankie gave me a somber look. "You don't know it, Kha, but the wasps in this business call me a 'mouser.' It's 'cause I'm Italian. Every mortgage broker gets creative with the Xerox machine from time to time, but me they call a mouser. They look over my loan aps ten times closer than any other guy's. And I still do better than any of them."

I could feel the quiet anger in his voice, and the bitterness. The only other time I heard him talk that way was about his father, a dock-worker who used to get drunk and beat his mother and sister.

"Don't worry, Kha,'" he said. "You'll get your loan."

The years went by and I stayed about even while he became more and more successful. And yet it was almost like he didn't know what to do with his money: He invested in a scam ruby mine in Burma. He blew 30 grand on a porno film that was so bad people laughed when they should have been getting horny. There was shrimp from Red China that spoiled before it got packed. And hardwood from the Philippines that ended up in the wrong port and was gone before they could trace it. A Portland area local lifestyle magazine that bombed. A rabbit ranch that went busted when the cute little hoppers died before they grew big enough to cut up for meat. We stayed in touch, mostly by phone, and he would joke about it. "If Billy knew half the stuff I've lost money on, she'd go through the roof!"

Not long after that, he started talking about doing another movie. He'd never lost the film bug, even though "Sexy Suburban Sluts" had been a big wash-out. And now he had gone and written a script without me.

He paid my way up to Portland, and the first draft was pretty weird, full of mysterious naked ladies and flying bells, and oboe solos portraying life and death. I don't mean it was bad. It was the kind of first film that cinema students shoot at UCLA Film School and maybe somebody sees it and they get their big break in the industry. Hell, Lucas, Coppola and Spielberg all started that way. I agreed to help expand it to feature-length. I would get to direct, and we would produce it ourselves. Frankie would come up with the money, and it would be my move into the big time.

That's when we formed Moon Air Productions. Maybe it was as impossible as lunar oxygen, but we were going to do it anyway. There was just one problem; as the script developed, I could see we weren't going to be able to shoot it as low-budget as we'd expected. Still, I figured, what the hell, we'd go down to the Hollywood mill and pitch it to the ghouls, same-same like everybody else, G.I. Frankie didn't say anything when I talked like that, just stared at me like I was from some other planet.

I was leaving for L.A., and he'd taken me to the airport. I remember I'd noticed how gray he was getting, how sad and preoccupied. Frankie was actually middle-aged! I never stopped to think that, for every line on his face, he must have been seeing two on mine. The words popped out before I really thought about it. "Are you okay, Frankie...?"

Usually he would have sloughed it off with that great laugh of his, but this time he didn't. "What do you mean?"

"Well - you've got a loving wife, a great kid, success. But lately you seem out of it somehow..."

"Kha... you did something really important for me once and now I – ahh, never mind." He started to turn away and then he turned to me again. "This film - it's a big reach, you know?" He looked at me like the world was in balance and he was waiting for some sign. A sign from me, his chum, the guy who saved his life in 'Nam.

Hey, the guy needed reassurance. I didn't think twice about it; I grinned and said, "Don't worry, old buddy. Money is your business. You'll get the money, somehow. Man's reach should exceed his grasp."

That smile lit up his face and he looked almost young again. "You got that one right, Kha!" he said. He gave me a big, affectionate hug and kissed me, Italian style, right there in the middle of the airport lobby. I turned red and my face and ears burned, and I got on the plane back down to L.A. with hardly a care in the world.

Things are quieter now, and I've got a lot of time to think about those days. I'm not even directing commercials any more. I'm back where I began, at the bottom of the ad business, writing mostly junk mail for a real estate guy. There's something pleasantly unconnected and even proper about the relationship, no questions asked, just move the houses, pal. It's a young man's game. Sometimes I joke about how old ad copywriters love cheap muscatel because it stops their hands from shaking, but that's just another lie. I really drink scotch, lots and lots of smooth and lovely scotch.

Yeah, I killed him alright, though at the time it was the last thing on my mind. Can you imagine it… once upon a time we were the Moon Air boys, two small-time hustlers who somehow thought we could make it to the big leagues. It seems so long ago and far away, like it happened in an old movie I saw on late-night TV, or maybe in a dream.

MAVIS MANYMONEY

Autumn 1962   Mavis Manymoney was some kind of witch. At least that's what she told people. It was the natural thing, the way they lived on the island of Jamaica, and her mom and granny and aunties had taught her everything they knew about the mumbo and the juju, the incantations, the stick-pin dolls and the rest of it. She lived in the same apartment complex as Beale, a U-shaped three story building with parking underneath, over on Strathmore in the village a few blocks off campus, and of course that sort of gossipy thing spread around pretty fast. She'd give you a predatory grin and ask for a fingernail clipping or if she could borrow your comb, just a few strands of hair was all she needed, and the way she said it, you couldn't be sure she was joking around or not. She said she kept other witches out with a trail of blessed sand spread across her doorway at night, and anybody walking past her place to their own could see the little trail of beach sand, spread out in a thin wiggly line, right there. With her hair-trigger temper and that grim faced stare of hers, folks in the apartment tended to give her plenty of space to go on and be as crazy as she wanted.

Unfortunately, Beale had been on her bad side since the first time they'd met. He'd been up on the rooftop deck practicing fencing with Janelle, an undergrad he was sweet on. Not that he knew that much about fencing, but Janelle was trying to make the university fencing team, and any old body would do. With his customary tenacity, Beale had read the right how-to books and gone into a personal training regimen. After a while, he'd improved to where he had to let her stick him every now and then so she wouldn't get too pissed off.

They were in the middle of one of those longish *six et quatre et six et quatre* bouts, rattling back and forth across the flat rooftop of the complex as the morning sun began to burn through the low hanging fog off the Pacific. Suddenly, the door to the stairway banged open and they were stopped mid-*quatre* by a screaming dervish with a thick layer of blue goop smeared all over her face, bright yellow crap on her lips and pink curlers in her hair. This fierce apparition of a girl was wearing only an open bathrobe that showed off her ebony black skin. She had a thin, but not unattractive body, and from what little Beale could make out of her face, it featured high cheekbones, a thin nose and a thin-set mouth made for frowning and disapproval. All in all, it was an astounding and unexpected entrance. Beale took off his mask, gaping at the semi-naked spectacle in front of him.

The newcomer screamed, waving her fists in the air and oblivious to the fact that she was charging at two people with fencing foils in their hands who could skewer

38

her like a barbeque chicken.

She yelled, "What are you crazy moron white peoples doing, stomping on the ceiling over my head in the middle of the night?"

Janelle sighed. "Mavis, it is ten in the morning. And be reasonable, this is a public deck."

"You got no right to be stomping on my roof, no time of day, bitch!"

It looked to be the beginning of World War III, but just as Janelle pulled off her mask and took a firmer grip on her foil, Mavis held up one hand like she was stopping traffic. She stared at Beale as if seeing him for the first time, looking him up and down like he was a popsicle or a candy bar.

"'Nilla Boy!" She purred, moving toward him like a big black cat. She reached out and stroked his cheek. "Sweet, delicioso 'Nilla Boy! Aww, now, here now, you skin so milky white and pretty..."

Beale took an involuntary step back, and the moment was interrupted as five of Mavis's house guests in various states of undress came boiling up from the floor below and spilled out onto the deck. Mavis raised a hand in their direction. "No, no, no, no, islander-comrades, I got this in control. We just about done here." She paused and then dramatically pointed at Beale. "'Cepting I ain't done with you, 'Nilla Boy. Fact is, we you-an'-me, we just about to begin!" And with a sweeping flourish she gathered her orange robe about her hips in a queenly fashion and in another few seconds was gone.

A week went by before Beale saw her again. He was on campus, on his way down the sidewalk steps that led from the Grad English Department past Pauley Pavilion.

"Hey, 'Nilla Boy, why so glum in the face, mon?"
Mavis was sitting on a bench next to a small cluster of
student activity sign-up booths. In a tight blouse and short
shorts she was hardly recognizable as the fierce
apparition that had interrupted his fencing session.

Feeling like a seed in the wind, he drifted over to sit
next to her. "Ahh, well…I've just been to see my advisor."

"What, you flunking out?"

"No, just the opposite. He wants to fast track me for a
doctorate."

"Woah, woah, woah, the man hands you the world on
a silver platter and you doing a *Gloomy Gus?*"

"It's not what I want. I came here to learn how to
write, not how to catalog dead people's old dead words."

"Well, 'Nilla Boy, you do what the man wants, he gives
you what you want."

"Not this time." Beale eyed her, liking the fact that her
nipples showed through her thin blouse. "Don't you wear
any underwear?"

"You always say what you think?"

"Usually. Don't you?"

"Course I do. But that no way to talk to a lady."

Beale smiled, thinking but not daring to say the words
loose lady. "Sorry. What are you doing here? Going to
sign up for cheerleading?"

"Nooo, the opposite. I'm here to tear things down."

"What things?"

"Everything. All of this. Do you know my friend,
here?" She put one arm through that of a middle-aged
man sitting quiet as a mouse next to her. The fellow was

chunky and balding, and reminded Beale of an accountant or some middle management flunky.

He waved a casual hand in Beale's direction. "Gus. Gus Hall." He turned to Mavis. "Bring him along tonight. We like disillusioned."

As Beale watched the man slowly get to his feet and walk away, his own mind was already back on his troubles.

All his professor wanted him to do was spend two or three years buried in the library stacks, researching possible connections between two English cleric poets. And Beale had turned the deal down.

"You're a fool, young Master Beale." The prof arched his eyebrows and looked down his nose at him. "You're throwing away your golden ticket to a life of academic ease and accomplishment."

"But I'm not interested in minor English poets from two or three centuries ago."

"Nobody cares what you want, Master Beale. Take it or take a hike."

Mavis was giving him an odd look. "You don't even know who that was you just met, do you, 'Nilla Boy?"

"Sure. Gus Bell. He said so."

"Gus *Hall*. *The* Gus Hall. The CPUSA."

"What's the CPUSA?" Beale asked.

She gave him a scornful look. "The Communist Party of the United States of America, you simple ignorant pure white 'Nilla Boy."

The meeting turned out to be a dismal flop. About fifty students turned out for a rally outside Raleigh Hall. There were a few posters on sticks with slogans that Beale didn't understand.

He was a half-hour late and Gus had come and left by the time he got there. Mavis furiously shoved a stack of pamphlets in his face. "Here 'Nilla Gorilla. Hand these out."

"What's wrong?"

"We arranged for a TV crew to show up. Channel 5. We paid the rotten bastards."

"You paid for a film crew?"

She looked at him like he was a moron. "How else you get them here?"

"Well, apparently it didn't work."

For a moment she looked like she might claw him, but something else distracted her and she angrily padded away.

The night air off the ocean had him shivering. He should have worn a warmer jacket. He found a spot out of the cold and examined the flyers she had given him. The headline read "Invader-gangster American Colonialists— Get out of Vietnam!" There was a picture of what looked like a World War II tank rearing up to crush some startled cone-hatted peasants working in a rice field.

Later that night, while sharing a big bottle of cheap jug red, Mavis started in on him about the deficiencies in his upbringing and education.

"You a know-nothing white boy from the house of privilege."

"And you?"

"Don't you start in on me, boss-man! Down in Kingston, me only 16, I see the policeman flunky of the colonials blow away my sister, one round pistol shot catch her in the eye."

"Yes, but I wasn't 'starting in on you,' as you say."

"Oh, yeah, that's what you say so, yeah. It always be the same. You here because you want some of this hot black mamma. That what you want, 'Nilla Boy!"

Her one-room apartment that generally was teeming with riffraff was deserted. She crawled across the pillow strewn floor and launched herself at him.

"Well, here I am!" They made love like wild animals; at least she did, while he did his best to keep up. And over the next few days when they weren't going at each other, they argued about the flaws of Western Civilization, the greed and corruptness of the so-called Democratic society, and the brighter better way that was coming.

"You don't know what the hell you are talking about," Beale shouted. "You've never been to a Communist country, and you sure as hell have never been to Vietnam!"

"I don't need eyeglasses to see black-and-white right in front of my face!"

He made the excuse that he was late for class, and stormed out like he usually did.

On his way over to campus, Dave, a friend of Janelle's fell in alongside him. "What, you give up on fencing lessons?"

"I don't know. That wasn't going anywhere fast."

"Hope you're using condoms with the black witch."

"Well, sure, of course. Why do you ask?"

"The bitch from Jamaica is on record saying she wants a white baby, *any white baby.*"

"So?"

"Well, you know Andy was hanging tight with her over the summer. He found somebody had punched needle holes in his Trojans. She hasn't used your bathroom, has she?"

Beale said she hadn't, except for a time or two. He still had that lingering worry she was going to get a few hairs from his brush and do her island spells on him. But later that day he did a condom check and there was a neat little hole through the plastic wrapper on every one of his packs. They were nearly invisible and he had to look really close to be sure. So right there he had a tremendous incentive to get out of town.

In later times, he often told literary agents and film producers he'd volunteered for Vietnam to see war for himself like his heroes Hemingway, Crane, Heller and maybe Mailer, and this much was true. But Mavis had fired anger in him he hadn't known existed. Americans as *Invader-Gangsters? What the hell was that all about?*

He was going to find out for himself, and he saw the way clearly before him, just one safe handhold after another. That afternoon, he drove his junk car west to Santa Monica where he signed up for three years in the U.S. Army.

"Three years, I can get language school, right?"

"Sure," the sergeant said. "Any special language?"

"I'd like French."

"Hey, why not?"

Six months later while Beale was grinding half way through his intensive language course in alien sing-song Vietnamese, he got a postcard from Dave that Mavis was now chasing some ethnically liberated white boy who wanted a brown baby as badly as she did, but so far, no luck. Still, considering how things turned out for him, there were times Beale was convinced the witchy lady had vapored up and sent some sort of gaseous rotten voodoo luck in his direction just for spite.

DOM'S PLACE

February, 1964.   Dirty Old Mary's voice carried over the six foot high cubicle walls like a foghorn. "Goddamn son-of-a-bitch dink bastards got away again! Last week we send in the B-52's from Guam and we bomb the shit out of the motherfuckers and here they pop right back up again!"

Beale stopped his translation exercises and tried to listen in. Lowly grunts, E-4 and below, weren't allowed to the Monday morning briefings. Somebody else was patiently explaining something about the Viet Cong being dug too deep underground, but the deep gravel-pitch voice interrupted, "Well, crap on that, if 500 pound iron bombs don't work, I say nuke the fuckers!"

The meeting broke up and about a dozen officers and civilians hurriedly made their way past Beale's desk, glad to escape the wrath for another week. One, a buck sergeant Beale didn't recognize, made a show of knocking Beale's red covered Hoa's Viet-English Dictionary off his desk.

"Hey! That was no accident!"

Bill Tilgarski looked up from the Playboy magazine hidden in his loose-leaf binder and muttered, "Watch it, Sergeant Asshole."

Beale retrieved his book, looking after the stranger, who turned back momentarily to give him the finger and an angry glare.

"What was that craziness all about?"

Harry Cone, the civilian head of his section, looked after the sergeant with a sad grin. "That craziness is Sergeant Hinkelby. He failed Dittybopper School."

Bill snorted, "Nobody fails Dittybopper School. It's Morse Code, for crap's sake. Boy Scouts learn it."

Cone, who was angling for a promotion, was working on relating to the troopers, "Well, Hinkelby froze when those dits and dots started rattling through his ears. After that he spent three years pushing paper and two weeks ago he re-upped for six more, hoping to get assigned to crypto so he could win his precious security clearance."

Bill waved his arms in the air. "Sheesh! He could have mine!"

Beale looked after the sergeant, still angrily retreating down the long hallway. "How is a guy who can't learn basic Morse Code ever going to learn to decode it?"

"Well, that's what Dirty Old Mary said. She tossed a fit and rejected his application."

Beale was looking at his Hoa's, retrieved from the floor with its front and back covers torn off.

"A little tape will fix that," Bill said, in a voice like that of a mother comforting a child with a broken plastic fire engine.

"But...why is he mad at me?"

"You're his replacement part," Harry said. "Dirty Old Mary asked for you."

Beale had seen her around, the messy-looking, grey haired old lady with the hunched over posture and the voice that belonged in a horror movie. Mary was a fixture at the Puzzle Palace, a legendary civilian employee who had been a secretary before the second World War, had seen first-hand the incredible Pearl Harbor blunder, had become indispensable because she knew too much and so was given the semi-official title of 'crypto teacher' and a job for life. Longevity, in her case, wasn't expected to extend very far into the future because she was a chain smoker who worked at her desk in a surrounding cloud of gray, one Lucky Strike dangling from her lips with two or three small upward climbing spirals in the ashtray at her side.

"Beale. Specialist Beale. Get the fuck in here." This from around the doorway.

Cone nodded toward her office. "She's not so bad. Go get her, boy."

After a week, Beale was chain smoking, too, though he preferred Camels, the brand his father had preferred right up until his hard and nasty cancer death.

"All the operational decode crap is low level," Mary was telling him. "Dirt simple. Captain Midnight decoder ring stuff."

She snatched the coverts he'd been working on from him. "Yeah. Backwards vowels, backwards consonants, vowels in back. This one, three consonants and then a

48

vowel, and so on. This one, vowels in front." In the time it took to glance at each one, she had seen the patterns and broken them.

"These guys are low level. Grade school educations. Don't worry, you'll pick it up in no time." She looked up at him with a warning glance and stifled a cough. "I'm not saying they are stupid, but consider their problems. They need a code they can change every couple days, every week at most. They want to change it before we intercept and decode and nail their asses. What the fuckers don't realize is, we're as interested in triangulating their location as in what the fucking messages actually –"

Her sentence was broken off by a bout of heavy coughing. Beale was tempted to pat her back, but she held him off with a baleful glare. After a few seconds and a drink of water from the pitcher at her side, she lit up another Lucky Strike.

"Why do you like Lucky Strikes?"

"Reminds me of the war," she said, giving the soft pack in her hand an affectionate squeeze. *"Lucky Strikes Goes To War!* That was the slogan, and they gave them to the men with their rations." She set down the cigarettes. "Of course, the fucking target was green on the ones the G.I.s got. Lucky Strike *Greens* go to war. Greens tasted worse than dried cow pies."

"Harry told us you were here for Pearl Harbor."

"Here?" She gave a little cough and paused as if she might be starting up again. After another sip of water she squinted at him past the line of smoke drifting up from her cigarette to join the general haze. "There was no here back then. Just a couple of people in a shabby little office in D.C.

"We saw the signs. We cracked the code. *East Wind Rain.* It was the goddamned-est thing. We were like children. We didn't know what we were doing. Here it is, a Friday and we know the Japanese are going to attack and all we can do is use a goddamn public telephone to contact Hawaii. So we do that, but one admiral is out horseback riding and a general is having a lawn party and nothing gets through. We finally send a goddam fucking Western Union telegram, which gets delivered to Pearl Harbor by a guy—a *Nisei,* to boot...there's a holy fucking iron clad irony for you—a Japanese American riding a bicycle to warn the ships that hell is on its way, only he is peddling along about six hours too late because the bombs are already raining down."

She looked sad and somehow regretful. "If I had been smarter. If I had thought to tell our assholes to send that telegram before we wasted all that time trying to get those fools on the telephone...maybe..."

She was staring at a small clear plastic cube with smudgy Ektachrome shots of two small kids on two sides and cats on the other.

"Your kids?"

"Naw. I got no kids. Nieces and nephews. Me, I'm married to the crypto..."

She waved him out of the room as she went into another coughing fit. Beale was half way back to his desk before she was able to take in a loud gasp of air.

Friday night Bill Tilgarski talked Beale into a trip to

Dutchman's Mill, a beer hall about twenty miles outside of Boomtown. Tilgarski drove his beat-up 53 Plymouth and they arrived during Beer Bash, contests where four or five men sitting around a table downed shot glasses of beer from pitchers supplied by the house. The Dutchman's was a big and rowdy hall with round tables and a small patch reserved for dancing. The jukebox was trumpeting *Walk right in/ Sit right down/ Baby let your mind roll on.* But the big attraction was the shot glass competition.

"Come on, Jackie-poo, let's live a little!" Bill pulled him over to a table where the next bash was about to start.

"A couple of Monterey Marys gonna try to prove their manhood!" a jeering voice hooted, and Sergeant Hinkelby slid into the last chair at the table.

Beale started to get up, but Bill held him back and said, loud enough to be overheard, "Dumb-ass Sarge is already three sheets to the wind. Don't worry, Jackarino-bear, he'll be the first one down!"

The Bash sounded deceptively easy, but with six men in the contest, each agreeing to down a shot of beer ten seconds after the last, getting plastered fast was guaranteed.

Twenty minutes into the contest, Hinkelby leaned in Beale's direction. "So what was it like at language school, Specialist? I heard the rumors. You have to be a fairy to get in, right?"

Bill, who was sitting in between the two of them, downed his shot and shook his head. "No, you have to be smart. That's why you didn't make the cut." He nudged Beale. "Ten seconds on you, buddy." Beale hurried to gulp his beer down.

"Horseshit. Everybody knows you gotta be a homo-**sex-ual** to go lingie."

"That why you wanted in?" Beale gave him questioning look.

Hinkelby flexed his arms and leaned forward to leap across the table, but the other four men hurried their shots and it was his turn again. He wasn't expecting his turn and in his hurry spilled half the glass.

"Re-do!" a passing waitress said.

Hinkelby snarled at her but he refilled his glass and just got it down before the buzzer sounded. He settled back in his chair, seeming to have forgotten his train of thought. In a few seconds he dozed off, and when his turn came again he was snoring.

The two Monterey Marys nearly made it to the end, but after two hours they could not find room for another ounce of Schlitz, and so they paid their share of the pitchers. As they staggered out to the parking lot, Bobby Bare was wailing on the blaring loudspeakers, *Last night I went to sleep in Detroit City/ And I dreamed about those cotton fields and home…* The night air was chill and their breath steamed out of their mouths.

Beale saw Sergeant Hinkelby sleeping behind the wheel in a sparkling new Ford Falcon.

Bill yelled, "Hey Sarge, you sleeping there all night?"

"You fucking sons-of-bitches!" Hinkelby started his Falcon, but lost sight of his tormenters, who jogged through the big lot to their own car.

Bill drove two blocks before they realized a desperate need to relieve themselves. They were in process when they heard the Falcon.

"Oh oh, here comes Hinky Dinky," Bill said.

But Hinkelby went roaring by, eyes set on the road ahead.

Five miles up the road, the sergeant was pulled to a dead stop just on the far side of four sets of railroad tracks.

Bill pulled to a stop right next to the Falcon and Beale yelled, "Sarge, you can't park there!"

Hinkelby woke with a start, but when he saw who it was, he yelled, "Get the fuck out of my life you homo queer lingies!"

That night Beale dreamed the Puzzle Palace was a huge barn-like place, a mammoth casino and beer hall with a big neon sign flashing on top that said DOM's Place. Inside the hall the waitresses all looked like Dirty Old Mary except they had young bosoms laced up in the front like the girls at the Dutchman's.

"Dreams mean something," he told Bill on their way over to the Palace.

"Yes, they do; they mean you are sleeping."

"No. I think Dirty Old Mary is a symbol. She's totally fucked up, but she understands everything, she solves everything, she knows everything. I tell you, if there's one person who stands for this entire operation..."

"Jackie-poo, you are a certified nutball."

That day Sergeant Hinkelby didn't show up for work, and about noon the word drifted around the department he was in the hospital. He showed up later in the day, banged up with dark bruises around his eyes, and with his arm in a sling.

Hinkelby sobbed like a kid as he told Harry Cone his

sad story. "My new Falcon stalled out on the tracks and no way I could get her started."

"Insurance should pay for that," Harry replied, the note of false sympathy clear in his voice.

"What insurance?"

"Oh, well, then maybe the car was a lemon. The dealership has to take it back. You just stop payment. You're heading back to the Far East in a few weeks. They'll have to come and get you."

"I can't," Hinkelby wailed. "I paid cash for the discount." His angry gaze wandered over to Beale's desk. "Bought it free and clear with the money I got for re-upping for six fucking years in this man's goddamn fucking army.

TEDDY POST'S WAR

Spring, 1985.   It is 40 years after his war, and Teddy Post still walks with a limp and an ebony cane with an ornate handle of solid gold, and when he's been on his feet all day you can see the pain in his eyes. But you don't say anything—nobody on the set dares say anything—because this is the same Ted Post who everybody knows nearly lost his leg on a beach in Italy in World War II. They know because Teddy tells them the story the first time they get together.

Right after his leg was nearly torn off by the shell fragments, they dressed him for pre-op, which means they swabbed him down with alcohol in the big olive drab canvas tent set up right there on the beach where they were hacking off limbs and stuffing guts back into stomachs. When the saw-bones bent over to have a closer look at Teddy's face, to see if this one might survive or not be worth the effort, the angry young man grabbed the doc's dog tags, staring hard at the name stamped there.

"If you cut off my leg," he said to the man he'd pulled close to his lips, "I'll spend the rest of my life until I find you. And then I'll hack your leg off."

"But you'll die if we don't," the doctor said, prying his dog tags from Teddy's fingers.

"I'd rather be dead. It's my choice. You do it my way."

"But your bones are all crushed."

"I'll just be a little shorter on that side," Teddy said.

That's the kind of guy he is, indomitable Teddy Post. Beyond that bit of legend he is a *bona fide* Hollywood legend, too, a director whose list of television and movie credits spans four generations. What director worked with Clint Eastwood on both Hang 'Em High and Magnum Force? What director did both the pilot show for Perry Mason and the pilot for Cagney & Lacey? What director has done Gunsmoke, The Fred Astaire Show, Twilight Zone, Peyton Place, and Colombo? Teddy Post, of course.

Beale heard about him through a monthly newsletter that came in his hillside mailbox from the Directors Guild of America. Though Beale made most of his money as a writer, he directed radio and television commercials through the guild.

There is not much need or opportunity for dramatic interpretation when the sub-text is always *Buy Our Product*, and so when Beale read that the legendary Ted Post was teaching a Master Director's Class, he called down to see if he could get in and learn something about *real* directing. The course was limited to 12, "by invitation only," and was already filled. But at the last minute they called back—somebody had dropped out and he was in.

Beale had lost his job bossing around the department that stuck together movie trailers at Disney Studios, and so he had plenty of time on his hands. There would be eight class sessions in all, four hours every Saturday morning for two months. In the eight weeks, each student would be expected to direct at least two dramatic pieces of 5 to 10 minutes in length, pieces that had two or more actors.

At that time he was working on a novel about four young Americans who join the army, get into military intelligence and end up in Vietnam. He thought it might be a good idea to take some scenes he'd written and try them out on the class.

He fished around for information on Teddy and found he'd directed Go Tell the Spartans, one of the few Vietnam War motion pictures that had been produced up to that time. Beale rented a VHS cassette, and it turned out to be a typical anti-war message movie. In fact, it seemed more stereotypical than most. Beale shrugged it off; it was the way Hollywood treated the things they thought they understood.

In the first story he developed for the class, four American soldiers who are cryptographer/linguists with top secret clearances are sent outside Saigon to work with Vietnamese Intelligence in a fairly unsecured area. The Americans spend their time fooling around and making fun of the war effort…but their mood changes once they realize their room is bugged.

Beale felt pretty solid about this scene because it was a recreation of something that had happened to him and several of his fellows back in 1964 when the angry ARVNs had just about dumped them somewhere way out in the bush. But Teddy Post and Beale's classmates jumped all over his story. Beale might have understood if they had attacked based on his lack of experience directing dramatic material; after all, he was only a director of commercials, and they seemed to tear apart everything everybody else did, anyway.

But Teddy didn't have a word to say about Beale's directing. He just kept muttering, "Soldiers just don't act that way."

Beale drove his Fiat Spyder through winding Topanga canyon, the tires screeching and the cold wind poking icy fingers through his flaring Prussian mustachios and his shoulder length hair as he tried to figure out just what had gone wrong.

He ran his VHS copy of Go Tell the Spartans again. It was the often retold story of what happens when a remote high command foolishly insists on building a distant outpost in an area where the enemy has massive strength. In Teddy's film, the distant outpost is saved from instant annihilation by the presence of old war hand Bert Lancaster, who recognizes doom is coming and prepares the men for the fight of their lives (deaths). The main characters are a gnarly officer (Lancaster) who has ruined his career by dropping his pants at the wrong time, a young sensitive writer-recruit, a smattering of drunks and dopers sure to "get theirs" when the shit comes raining down, and a handful of inscrutable Vietnamese "friendlies" who either prove to be loyal or deceitful. Watching Teddy's movie, Beale kept thinking *What the hell's wrong with MY stuff?!* After that, he didn't see any reason to just sit back, he decided he was going to charge full tilt ahead.

It took a full week's effort to prep a scene, but Beale had the advantage, he was "on hiatus," the Hollywood euphemism for "out of work." After selecting what he wanted to do, there was casting, blocking out the action, and rehearsals. It was a lot of preparation, and for very little reward; his classmates tore each other's work apart with abandon. After the first class, there were openings every week. Maybe they didn't have the time, or maybe they weren't so eager to get their own stuff up on the stage. Whatever, Beale saw his opening and took it. He had a scene ready every week. Some weeks he was the only person ready and able to go.

And he was learning. Teddy was showing him a hundred things; how to pull down an actor who was dominating the scene when he wasn't supposed to, how to shift the mood and the tempo, how to color the scene to make it say what you wanted.

He could handle the class putdowns, but Teddy's attitude still bothered him. Teddy sat there tapping his thumbs on his cane and frowning at the antics of Beale's characters. Beale wondered, was he being too presumptuous, performing his own stuff instead of scenes from *The Glass Menagerie* or *Death of a Salesman*? Did he have some terrible blind spot? Was his stuff just plain *bad?* Maybe there was some truth in all of that, but he kept coming back to Teddy's reaction to his first piece. *Soldiers just don't act that way.*

For his final piece, Beale developed a scene to take place in the so-called *Puzzle Palace,* the top secret intelligence headquarters of the National Security Agency. He had spent six months in that topsy-turvy place and thought he had a powerful idea that somehow related to the insanity, foolishness and waste of the day-to-day operations of the war he had experienced.

In his scene, there has been a tragic, yet amusing, incident. A drunken sergeant has fallen into a giant pulper used to dispose of the tons of top secret waste paper that must be discarded every day. In fact, Beale's characters were present when the sergeant was ground into a big bale of waste paper, and they have feelings about this tragi-comic event ranging from a casual shrug to horror to a haunting sense of guilt.

Beale's actors completed the scene without a hitch, even though it was complicated and somewhat longer than the previous ones he'd done. There was the usual stunned silence, and then hands shot up all over the room.

Beside Teddy, Beale had one other nemesis in the class, a ram-rod straight assistant director who said he'd been in Vietnam almost eight years. This guy's hand shot up like a gun. Teddy ignored the others and nodded in his direction.

"The problem with this piece," the assistant director said, "is that I don't like any of these soldiers. I don't have anybody to cheer for."

"I didn't know I had to direct them *likeable,*" Beale shot back.

"Well…believable, then. I was there, and I don't think they're believable."

"That's just your experience. You're pretty unbelievable, yourself."

"How's that?" The assistant director looked genuinely puzzled.

"Well, you started as a private and ended up as a Captain."

"What the hell difference does that make?"

"You're on the side of discipline and rigidity and the war effort."

"That's dumb!"

"I don't think so," Beale said. "Suppose you'd started as a captain and had your ass busted to corporal, maybe just due to some unlucky moves you made, the wrong place at the wrong time, that sort of thing. I'm sure you might have a little more sympathy for my characters."

There was a titter from the class. The guy looked like he was going to say something else, but thought better of it and sat down.

Teddy cleared his throat from the back of the room. "I agree with the criticism. This is the same as the other war scenes you've done. These characters aren't believable."

This may have been the prestigious Director's Guild of America's Master Directorial Class, but Beale had had it with his famous Master Director.

"Sorry, Teddy. I really don't know what the hell you're talking about, and I don't think you do, either."

This was tantamount to Mutiny on the Bounty. Directors have the biggest egos in the world; a director on his set is the next thing to God Almighty, and Teddy treated his class like he was at the helm of Gone with the Wind.

The old director's face got red and he lurched to his feet, waving his cane in Beale's direction like it was the barrel of an M-1 rifle. "You're not the only one who knows about Vietnam!!" he thundered.

"I didn't say I was. I said I don't know what you're getting at. You keep saying the same things, but I don't understand them."

"Goddamn it, I know all about war! I was in World War II! What the hell do you think this cane is about?!"

"Yes, Teddy, you charged up the beach in that splendid great war. You told us. You tell everybody."

"Oh, you think I don't know Vietnam? Is that what you think?! You young idiot, I directed what is arguably the best movie about Vietnam to this date! And I tell you, soldiers don't act the way yours do!! The way they mouthed off to that officer?! They'd have been in the brig—or shot!!"

"Right, the soldiers you knew didn't act that way—not in *your* war, Teddy. The war to save the world from Hitler. That wasn't the 'Nam war."

"The army doesn't change that much!"

"How do you know? You haven't been in the army in four decades."

Teddy's voice was close to the top of its register. "You don't have to go to Vietnam to know about Vietnam!"

"Well, it helps, Teddy. It might have helped you in that dumb-assed 'Nam movie you made."

My other nemesis, the assistant director, who had been steaming over Beale's comments, leapt to his feet. "Maybe your war experience *narrowed* your opinion rather than broadening it!"

"Right. The real thing makes you ignorant. Where do you come up with this stuff?"

"It could have…" he said in a low voice. But after that he sat down and shut his mouth.

It was Beale's turn to rant. "All I know is, I went and saw for myself. Maybe I picked the wrong war, but it wasn't like Crane's war, it wasn't like Conrad's war, it wasn't like Hemingway, it wasn't like Heller—and it certainly wasn't like Teddy Post's war!"

Teddy glowered at Beale. "Well, tell us, Mr. Big Time War Expert, what was it like?" From the look on his face, Beale was glad they weren't taking the course for a grade.

"It was like my scenes! My war is staring you in the face and you can't see it!"

The squabbling went on a while longer, but Beale pulled back from it when he realized there wasn't going to be any resolution. In his experience, there never was when Americans got to chewing over the deadly disagreement in Southeast Asia that had been going on for centuries before the Americans got there.

The conversation drifted to other things. Teddy ignored Beale while he did a review and a wrap-up of the class accomplishments. Beale sighed and fixed his gaze on his instructor's gold handled cane that leaned forgotten against the Master Director's chair. It was time to move on.

GOOD TIMES AT
THE HAPPY JACK PLATTER SHOP

Spring, 1965. Beale made a series of overlapping water rings on the slick black Formica with his damp beer glass while sneering, glaring and grinning at his crooked reflection in the mirror tiles behind the bar. The tiles were small and so his reflected image was warped and strange, and made weirder by the yellow and green neon tube lighting that was set in a rim around the bar top in a way that glowed to give patrons the look of demons or space aliens.

He was doing his drinking and forgetting on a stool in a very busy bar on the Street of Flowers near what used to be the prosperous downtown business section of Saigon. He'd had a few close calls lately, plus the news that Grace Ann, his old stateside girlfriend might be in the process of dumping him. He was dressed casual, in slacks and a polo shirt. He had checked out from the orderly room in the afternoon and taken a *xe hoi* taxi downtown. It was two days before payday and so the bar was nearly deserted.

"You buy for me one Saigon Whiskey?" a pleasant voice lisped in his ear. She was his designated bargirl, making the rounds, and he was in a drinking mood.

"Okay, why not? One more beer for me."

"Howrrrrr you doin', mon?" A thick-burred voice said from a barstool a few spaces on down the neon.

Beale wheeled around on his barstool, wobbling a little.

"What's that you shay?" His lips were numb; the effect of formaldehyde in the local brew.

"Howrrrr you doin', mon?" the fellow repeated.

"What are you, Scotch or something?"

"Scotsman," he corrected Beale. "I hail from Aberdeen, Laddie." He looked to be in his mid-thirties, a short and stocky man, ruddy-faced, with a bristly brush of reddish blond hair shooting from the top of his head.

"I mean, how did a Scots-man get over here?"

"Oh, I came by plane, lad." He looked sadly into his glass.

"Let me buy you one. What are you drinking?"

"Stout." The man gave Beale a quick once-over. "So, ye'r in the army, now?" It was only half a question and not a very difficult guess. Of the Americans in Vietnam at that time, 95% of them were soldiers.

"Yes. I'm...a clerk."

Beale wasn't a clerk, but he couldn't say anything different. There were rules against it.

"Well, how'd jer like to take over me job?"

"And what might that be?" Beale asked politely.

"I'm a rrrrrrrradio jock, mon!"

"A what?"

The bargirl brought the stout, another beer for Beale, and her own Saigon Whiskey. He usually paid 15 piasters for *Ba Muoi Ba* and 50 P for her tea. He gave her a two hundred P note and waved her away. He couldn't concentrate on the notes; they were colored like Monopoly game money and seemed next to worthless. He stared at the dragon watermark on a green-and-red 5 P note on the bar.

There was that burr again. "I said, I'm a rrrrradio jock, mon!"

"I don't listen to the radio much." Beale hadn't listened once since dropping down out of the sky into South Vietnam.

"I do a morning show over at VTVN, ya know, the native station."

"In Vietnamese?" Beale asked, staring at the fellow in amazement.

The Scotsman blinked his light blue eyes as if he'd been struck on the forehead with a thousand-year-old egg, the sulfurous, rotten ducks eggs lined in a row behind the bar, waiting for the next American fool to prove his manhood.

"No, course not. Sing-songy, bird-chirpy Vietnamese?! Are ye daft? I speak in the King's English, mon!"

"Well, I speak English and I can hardly understand you."

The Scotsman didn't take offense. He grinned. "Nobody else in Saigon can either, laddie. I told you, it's a *native* station, VTVN Radio Saigon. The head of the station doesn't speak any English at all. He thinks everybody speaks like me."

"That's incredible," Beale muttered.

"Well, how about it?"

"About what?"

"It's a half hour show. You do the news, play a song or two, chatterrrr it up a bit. It's a good job, 5,000 P a week."

"Then why are you quitting?"

"I'm leaving in three days for the highlands, mon."

"Central Vietnam?" Beale's interest perked up. He had never been out of Saigon, but, like all army-trained Vietnamese linguists, he wanted to see the ancient capital city of Hue.

"No, mon. The Scottish highlands!" The Scotsman laughed and bought Beale another beer. "Come on, mon, I promised them I'd find somebody. This is the beginning of your carrrrrreeerrrrrr in rrrrrrrradio!"

The thing was, Beale said to himself, he could do this. Of course, the C.O. would shit a brick if he ever found out, but like the crazy Scot said, it was *native* radio. Nobody listened to the show, except maybe a few misguided University of Saigon students, hoping to hone their English skills and win a non-existent exemption from the obligatory three-plus-three-plus-three years in the military service.

Beale was already teaching a morning English class at the Hoi Viet My, the Vietnamese-English school. He'd just have to get up a little earlier, get off-base and downtown to the radio station.

The next morning he ran naked through the hazy predawn light to the screened off showers. He carried a towel in one hand and with the other held his possibles kit over his head to keep the warm rain out of his hair. Somewhere nearby the shuddering flup-flup-flup of two or three HU-1bs sounded. Davis Station was right next to the Tan Son Nhut airport runway, with a helicopter unit on one side and a patch of swampy land on the other.

Beale was thinking he was crazy to go through all this trouble for nothing. He'd had a lot of beers; maybe he'd imagined it. Maybe the Scotsman was drunk, stringing him along. Maybe he wouldn't show.

Still, maybe he would. Beale showered and threw on some damp civvies. The rainy season had started and it was impossible to be really dry in the normal sense. He signed out and stood in front of the gate at the 3rd Radio Research Unit with a copy of Vit!Vit! over his head. Vit!Vit! one of the dozens of Saigon newspapers printed every day. Beale read them constantly, trying to improve his skills in Vietnamese, which were weak for someone in his position, but they also worked as crude umbrellas. He was a linguist/translator and a cryptographer, with a Top Secret security clearance. His job was decoding and translating covert Viet Cong messages, but in the rainy season, intercepts dropped to almost zero and he wasn't very busy. He wasn't supposed to be moonlighting, he wasn't supposed to be teaching school, and he wasn't ever supposed to be in an unsecured area... there were a lot of things he wasn't supposed to do. Being in Vietnam was scary... he'd already been shot at, and, but for a chance of fate, would have been wounded or killed in an explosion at the airport restaurant. On the other hand, you only live once. This was a chance to see another facet of Vietnam, and he was going to take it. The cyclo-bus splashed down the rut spotted road and pulled to a stop in front of him. Beale crawled in back with three *ba's* heading for the Saigon market.

"Chao, *Ba*," he said, inclining his head respectfully to the ladies.

"Chao, Anh," the lady nearest him said with a broad smile. It was no secret the soldiers at the 3rd RRU spoke Vietnamese and did secret things with radios. She continued in Vietnamese, "Are you married, young man?" She couldn't have been more than forty. She expertly spat a thick stream of bright orange Betel nut juice over the side of the little bus. She carried a live chicken, legs bound with twine. Upside down, the bird strained its neck and eyed Beale, looking for food.

"No, not yet," Beale replied.

"Then you must marry my daughter," the woman said, patting the swollen stomach of a young girl seated next to her. Beale's face reddened and the crowd of ladies broke into merry laughter.

Fortunately he was rescued by their arrival at the main gate. Beale bid his goodbyes, careful not to let the upside down chicken peck him.

He slept in the cab as the driver wove and shouted his way down Pasteur Street to the radio station. Wonder of wonders, the ebullient Scot was there, just like he said he'd be. He walked Beale around and introduced him as their new radio personality.

"Here's where we pick up the news, mon." He shoved some scraps of paper in Beale's hand. Then he dragged his new apprentice into the booth, clamped a set of earphones over his own ears and a second set over Beale's and they were on the air.

With the headphones on, Beale felt oddly lonely and confined. He was in a small, soundproofed booth with tinny sound coming in his ears and a big silvery microphone a few inches away from his lips, the world waiting to receive the wisdom of his pronouncements. His throat was dry; he had no business being here. A scratchy version of the William Tell Overture was playing in his ears, followed by a canned announcer welcoming listeners first in Vietnamese and then in heavily French-accented English to the Nha Vo Tuyen Truyen Thanh, VTVN, Radio Saigon. The music dipped down. Outside the window glass, a native girl dressed in an ao dai smiled and pointed in at them. The Scotsman gestured to Beale, indicating the scraps of copy in his hands.

"What?" Beale said.

"We're on the airrrrr," the Scotsman said. He pointed furiously to the scraps of news.

Beale looked at them. The sentences had sections blackened with thick black lines. Other parts were snipped out, leaving holes in the paper. He started, "Ahh, today American President Linden B. Johnson said... good crops were indicated for the Hawaiian pineapple industry, agricultural spokesman said... and — a sad note — Thornton W. Burgess, the author of the much loved Peter Rabbit stories, died at the age of 91...the Gemini 4 flight that was successfully launched from Cape Kennedy,

Florida... is in the second day of a four-day flight... there is a proposed space-walk..."

He went on like that for five minutes, and as Beale saw no one was stopping him, his voice came down from the hesitant tenor register to something slightly more newscaster-like. The Scotsman was beaming him an I-told-you-so smile, and, after the broadcast and a handshake in the giant marble floored lobby of the station, he hailed a cab and was gone forever. Beale was a radio announcer, with his own show.

This was a couple of years before Adrian Cronauer had his Good Morning, Saigon show, and Beale wasn't on Air Force Radio, either. This was the real thing, VTVN – native radio. After a few weeks, he came to look forward to their signature, the scratchy 78 rpm of the William Tell Overture somebody had swiped from the Canadian Broadcasting System. It was an odd meeting of technology and superstition. The two girls who worked the show expertly spun the big black platters and turned the dials as if they knew what they were doing. But they wore slit-skirted ao dai rather than Western clothing, and they ducked under the table whenever they heard the low rumble from the B-52's shellacking the provinces, convinced it was the ghosts of their dead ancestors.

After a while, he thought he should put his own individual stamp on his show. He took a cab over to the downtown PX just off of Hai Ba Trung Street where he found a recording of Mancini's bubbly Elephant Walk. He would use that as his show signature, a symbol of the jazzy and indomitable American spirit. The Americans had landed, the Americans were here, everything was going to be all right. The station director shrugged and went along with it. If Mancini wanted his usage royalties, he could come and get them.

Beale called his show <u>The Happy Jack Platter Shop</u>. He would read the news, and then have the girls spin records that he mostly scammed from G.I. buddies. The news was a little complicated, though the stories came clacking off the teletypes from AP and Reuters just like they do in newsrooms around the world. But at VTVN, they had Vietnamese government interpreters who translated everything to Vietnamese, then manually snipped out offending passages, and the remainders were tossed back to the station interpreter, Mr. Van Nguyen, who translated them back into mind-numbing, chop-sock English.

Beale had to rely on the very serious Mr. Van Nguyen, a man in his late-thirties who confided he was looking for his big break in the news game. He was very good at sticking together the pieces, but still, much of it was nonsense. When Van Nguyen was finished, Beale would have about 20 desperate minutes to smooth the most obvious craters, and then he was on the air.

Beale had known Van Nguyen for about a week when the little guy with his heavy dandruff, sour-whiskey-and-cigarette breath and small potbelly hanging over the belt-line of his truly cheap suits started bugging him for a Pentax.

"I could be happy even with the smaller Pentax," he pleaded in desperate, wheedling tones, "the less expensive one without the wonderful zoom lens that would most certainly make my career in reporting…"

Beale stared at the wall where a picture of a sitting Buddha was taped, while Van Nguyen pressed his case.

"I know everybody asks you for things all the time, but this one camera and I will never, never bother you for anything more from the PX, except if perhaps you are going anyway, possibly some hair spray for my wife and maybe a few Hershey chocolate bars for my kids..."

Beale was managing to keep his temper, but just barely.

The morning the weak Phan Uy Quat government was overthrown, the Tan Son Nhut air base went to Orange Alert. For a while Beale thought he wasn't going to be able to do his show, but he managed to slip out just before the Orange became official. He could see the M.P.s behind him stopping G.I.s and making them turn around and go back to their units. Outside the gates, the *xe hoi* cabbies were still running – Beale heard after the fact that they had run right through the *Tet* Offensive, business as usual – and so he was able to flag a ride over to the station. It was a different city... he passed ARVN tanks in the streets and machine gun nests at corners that some military genius had decided were strategic.

The newsroom was deserted, but there was a stack of neatly clipped translations on Beale's desk. If possible, they were even more nonsensical than ever:

[blank space] farm crops [blank space] the cooler weather. [enormous blank space] resulting in lower prices.

[blank space] new American comedians [big blank space]

Nothing at all about the collapse of the government.

Still, Van Nguyen had clearly been and gone. *At least he wasn't going to have to listen to the little man's miserable whining about the camera he wasn't going to get.* It wasn't that Beale hated the guy; he was tired of Vietnamese sticking their hands out and asking for things. The minute you got to know a bargirl or a pedi-cyclo driver or a milkshake girl along the runway or a waitress at Chez Brodard's, practically the minute they knew your name, the hand was out for perfume, hairspray, radios and cameras from the PX.

Beale poured himself a bitter cup of coffee, scooped up the tattered copy and headed for the seclusion of the announcement booth. Before he knew it, William Tell was jangling in his ear, and then he was picking his way through the news. He turned the cut up farm story into another informative discussion of the pineapple industry, and went on to do a color piece on the Smothers Brothers, those happy, bumbling folk-singer comedians.

Hey, no problem, this show was nearly in the bag. Beale had his feet up and was into the music side of The Happy Jack Platter Shop – Peter, Paul and Mary were singing "Lemon Tree" – when a squad of ARVNs burst through the door into the room where the turntables and the jittery *co gai* were and started waving their machine guns around in the air.

It was a frightening, uncertain moment. They looked like boy soldiers who should have been in high school. They certainly shouldn't have had the carbines and light machine guns they were waving around. One of them figured out the magic of the soundproof double doors and made his way into the booth where Beale was sitting, frozen in fear.

The young soldier waved his machine gun at the ceiling and said in almost inaccessible English, "You say Ong Quat a filthy pig?"

"Ahhhhhh....nooooo....," Beale replied.

This didn't seem to make him happy. Beale figured it probably was the wrong answer.

"You say Ong Quat a filthy pig?" the kid-soldier repeated, turning the machine gun in a somewhat more operational way toward Beale's face.

"Ahhhh, maybe I did say something..." Beale stammered, throwing his hands in the air.

The soldier's face darkened and he slammed the safety off. Beale could see he hadn't been to Buddhist Patience School.

And then, by some miracle, the wonderful little Van Nguyen was there, stepping in between the two of them. He went on for a while in his sing-song way, arguing and gesturing with the kid, and then he turned to Beale.

"Mr. Beale, sir. A small mistake, sir." He shrugged. "This youngster with gun here, he want you to say Ong Quat is a filthy pig." Van Nguyen gestured encouragingly toward the mike, which was clicked off because Peter, Paul and Mary were still singing. "He not know we on air or not."

"Ohhhh..." Beale said, clearing his throat as he stumbled back into his chair.

While Peter, Paul and Mary sang about the sorrows of bittersweet love, Beale went to the closed mike and poured out his heart against that rat-dictator Phan Hui Quat, a man about whom he knew almost nothing.

"He is a rotten—err, pig of a dictator, a rotten—err, pig, not fit to rule, not a man, I say, but more of a pig, yes a pig of a man..."

The young soldier nodded in satisfaction, grinning every time he heard the word 'pig' linked to the hated Mr. Quat. The direction seemed to be working, so Beale rolled with it until Lemon Tree was over. Then he signaled the co gai outside to go directly to his end-tag of Elephant Walk.

"And this is Jack Beale, signing off once again for The Happy Jack Platter Shop where everybody's happy all the time..." Here he clicked his mike off again. "...and that pig Phan Hui Quat is a dirty rotten pig..."

After the show, one of the kids in khaki took a group shot of them with his battered little Kodak, and Beale even signed an autograph on the back of a crumpled napkin. He waved goodbye and walked swiftly down the big marble staircase. And then he was out the front door and hailing a cab, just happy to still be sucking air.

That afternoon – and he would have done it sooner, but the PX didn't open until noon – he ran over and bought his dear friend Van Nguyen his Pentax. Not the cheap model – the expensive one with the big black zoom hanging on the front that just might make his career. And some hair spray, and chocolate bars for the kids.

THE DANCING NAZI

August 1981.   Beale's answering service relayed
that he had a call from a Mr. Bill Tilgarski. Mr. Tilgarski
was currently residing at the Veterans Administration
Hospital on Wilshire Boulevard in Santa Monica and would
very much like to see him. All Beale had that day was one
of those low-budget cheapie movie pitch meetings at a
Denny's Restaurant, so after the boys from Manila
finished picking his brains, they politely shook hands and
bowed, which was Pacific Rim show biz shorthand for *So
long, American asshole.*

Beale piled into his aging MG sportster and rumbled
west on Sunset in the general direction of Santa Monica.
He was ambivalent about going to see Bill; he knew he
should be showing his face at the ad agencies about town
to stir up some new business, but he and Wild Bill had
gone through a year at language school together and had
some interesting times at Fort Meade on the East Coast
until Bill lost his security clearance. He remembered the
old Chinese curse, *may you live in interesting times.*

The Wilshire VA had the gloomy smell of the hopelessly maimed and terminally mangled. But Bill, to Beale's pleasant surprise, was sitting up, cheerfully reading the LA Times. While his old army chum had dark circles under his eyes, he was clean shaven and his big yellow mane was tossed back like it had been in the good old days, a la Elvis.

"Mister Hollywood, himself!" Wild Bill boomed, and Beale remembered that same voice thundering *Fuuuuuuck the Aaaaaaa-rrr-myyyyyyyy!* before the system had caught up to him and crushed him.

"Jeez, Wild Billy, I thought I'd find you in a coma or something."

Bill grinned. "Hell, Jackie-poo, it's early. They don't send the meds cart around until noon. Don't worry, I promise I'll be a zombie before three."

Beale pulled up a chair. "Can I get you anything?"

"Nah. I got everything I need here."

"Well, what happened? Last thing I remember, I got your invite; you were getting married. Sorry I couldn't come, by the way. Location shoot in Arizona."

Bill waved off his apology. "Hey, doesn't matter. That marriage didn't last, anyway. In a way, that's how I landed up here."

"I didn't know you were here."

"Well, I didn't exactly want to advertise. *Hey, your old pal Mister Crazy has gone off the deep end again.*"

"So you been here a while?"

"Almost a year now. It was, oh Christ, late-September or about that, anyway, as best I can remember. I was in my living room, belting down a brewski and yelling at the stupid Ram offense when the idiot police chopper came over with those big blades going flup, flup, flup, and I zapped up the sound because LA was only winning by six and it looked like Green Bay might steal it. There was enough going on; I didn't need the hassle when Sherry started yelling from the kitchen, 'Goddamn it, Billy, turn that fucking thing down, I'm on the phone with Mom!'

"Worse luck, my good friend Beale, I didn't catch what my dear sweet Sher was saying and next thing she threw a plate that smashed into a thousand pieces and that made me mad because it was our good plates and so I winged a shot to her head with the first thing I reached for, which happened to be a small vase, only she's got so much hair she probably didn't even feel it.

"Problem was, it was the blown glass purple one she got from Disneyland, so, her turn—she chucked the roast clear across the room *Kabamm!* right through the TV!

"If you'd have told me what a frozen hunk of meat could do to a TV screen, I'd never have believed you! The game went in a puff of smoke, and I never did find out if the Rams hung on.

"I probably would have killed her, but just then the chopper did a second daisy-chain overhead, so I went a little crazy and took the channel zapper outside and started shooting over the ratty palm trees, making like I'm back on some landing Z, *bam, bam, bam, BAMM!* In-coming, you mudder-fuckers, *IN-COMING!!* Of course, the neighbors started their pussy-foot wailing about the noise and somebody called the cops — well, it was grief like you don't want to know, and that was the night Sherry said she was leaving for the last time, and she did, too."

Wild Bill hitched himself up in his bed. "Which brings us to Fred's kid's wedding."

"It does?" Beale gave him a puzzled look. "You're losing me here, pal."

Bill gave him his classic wide grin. "Patience, oh ye of little faith, and all will be revealed. Fred was my neighbor-guy from Austria."

"Fred from Austria."

"Right. He worked steady for years for a big aerospace firm while I was getting laid off from the post office or this or that and just barely managing to hang onto our little shack next door. I'd be churning out screenplays about the 'Nam that nobody wanted, while coo-coo clock Fred would be merrily building decks or pruning his little orchard."

"I never knew you were writing screenplays."

Wild Bill gave him a wry smile. "Sure, I'm just an imitation Mister Hollywood. Took some night courses at UCLA. See, Beale, you're the real thing, my inspiration, actually, in a way..."

"You should have aimed higher, picked an Alfred Hitchcock or somebody like that."

"Well, you were the only guy in show biz I knew. Anyway, I'd get writer's block and storm out of my crappy little office to cuss and pull at the crabgrass and dandelions on my side of the fence. Fred didn't have weeds, he had roses and geraniums and duck weathervanes with spinning wings — and he'd come over with a couple of those heavy German brewskis and we'd sit on a ledge and talk about nothing for a while until I cooled down.

"I don't know why I ended up going to the wedding. Maybe I figured it would keep my mind off Sherry. Anyway, it turned out real coo-coo clock like I knew it would, Fred's kid standing at the altar of this white-washed Lutheran chapel like a plastic K-Mart prince next to his pretty pale blond bride. The ring boy and flower girl were right out of Hansel and Gretel and I slipped a couple of downers and shuddered a little as the icy I-don't-give-a-damn feeling started somewhere in the back of my brains."

"You were doping out at your neighbor's kid's wedding."

"Sure. Just a little, to hold off the boredom and the madness. The party was one of those catered, striped-tent affairs. As the local literary genius, I got a favored position next to Fred's boss's wife, but we ran out of conversation when I called Joyce Oates a pretentious smut-slut."

"You smooth talker, you."

"That aside, the affair was nice, in a way. Pretty girls in short frocks wandered around filling our glasses. Each table had mint candy and baskets of old-fashioned cookies, and a live five-piece band wheezing away at old favorites like *The Beer Barrel Polka*.

"Anyway, here I was having a time when I saw this amazing old guy, maybe in his seventies, dancing like a Fred Astaire who majored in polkas. This guy was really something! Trim, you know. Blond hair turning grey. Light on his feet. He would glide across the floor, snapping his fingers, clapping his hands and tapping his loafers heel-toe-across, and the plump, red-faced *house-*

fraus couldn't keep up with him."

"I always thought the polka was a clunky dance."

"Well, it isn't, not when you do it right. Still, it was stupid of me; I mean, I should have been heading home for the big crash and here I was watching an old kraut-head dancing the polka, for Christ's sake!

"The medley finished and he snagged a champagne from a pretty *fraulein* and headed for his own table, which was in my direction. Everybody clapped and cheered and I shouted, 'Far OUT, man!'

"I started it, you see. It was me, started it, just like always..." Bill looked like he was going down under a swarm of sad old memories, but then he resurfaced and grinned at Beale. "Hey, remember Dirty Old Mary?"

"How could I forget? Taught me everything I know about crypto."

"*Lucky Strikes Goes To War!* Looked like a cross between everybody's mom and a frog. Dirty Old Mary always did like you best, Jackie-poo. You know, that old bitch got me in a lot of trouble after you left for the show."

Beale knew that part of Bill's story. "Ah, Billy, you've been telling me you were at a wedding where old people were dancing."

"Right, right! Fred's kid's wedding! Sorry, sorry, I got off the track there... Well, like I'm saying, I gave a big shout out for the geezer dancer and his thin old face broke out with a big ear-to-ear, and he plopped into the empty chair next to me. 'Too old,' he said to me, 'but still, I wear out three or four women tonight!' Hell, he was mighty impressive for an old fart!

"Like a lot of Fred's guests at the wedding, this guy

had a German accent. You know, Beale, not too long ago there was such a thing as a German community in America. I know this because I'm a closet-German myself. My grandparents were all from *der Fatherland*."

Beale scratched his head. "I don't know, Billy-boy. Tilgarski sounds Polish to me."

"That's one of our secrets. I'll tell you what happened to the real German community in America; they started to disappear around World War I and they went nearly invisible once Hitler's Angels started tearing up Europe. They changed their names from Weiss and Schwartz to White and Black — and by the way, from Tiller to Tilgarski — and today about the only place you see them in the states is in the German deli hunched over the braunschweiger and Black Forest ham, solid blond people muttering things that sound like *dumpkaupft* and *alfeterzein*."

"Huh. I did not know that."

"Of course not. How could you? The very definition of the word *secret*. Anyway, one of the wine-girls came by and I looked at the luscious bare tops of her laced-up breasts and motioned to our glasses. The old man nodded his approval and I asked, 'Where'd you learn to dance like that?'

"Jackie-poo, he gave me a crisp, intelligent look that surprised the hell out of me. His eyes were lighter than blue, grey really, with gold flecks in them.

'In my native village,' he tells me. 'In Yugoslavia.'

'Ahh. You are Yugoslavian, then?'

'I am an American, like you.'

"You see that, don't you, Jack-ster? He was mocking

me, as if I'd asked him a child's question. Us secret Germans in America are good at mockery.

'But, your accent—" I tried to protest, but the old guy just waved that one off. The band interrupted with a medley of old standards, starting with *Has Anybody Seen My Gal.*

"The old man gave this new musical selection a disdainful sniff and settled back in his chair.

'What is your question?' he asked.

'Your accent. You have to be German.'

'Northern Yugoslavia was part of the empire.'

'Right. My great grandmother was from Celji. Do you know it?'

'Of course I know it,' he said, as if he'd just passed through that tiny and remote mountain village last week.

'So... what are you doing in Southern California?'

'Living life, just like you! What else is there to do?'

'Well, sure... but, how did you get here?' "Beale, this guy eyed me seriously for the first time, you know, gave me the gimpy eye — and then he asked me the question you hear from the German community in America, and perhaps at German communities around the world. He asks me, 'You're not Jewish, are you?'

'No. Of course not.'

'Good. I hate Jews. Jews and Russians.' His eyes twinkled. 'You're not Russian, are you?'

'Do I look Jewish or Russian?'

'No. You look like a beatnik. A... Vietnam War hero, I should say more precisely.'

'Yeah. Hero.' He must have seen something in my face, because he reached over and patted my arm like he understood everything about it. 'Your side picks you, you know. You have to accept it.'

'No. I picked my side!' I pulled my arm away and replied with a force that surprised even me. From across the table, the boss's wife gave me a dirty look.

"The old man frowned, and the wrinkles at the corners of his eyes deepened as he looked at me. Then he said, 'I was a Nazi, you know.'

'How did you get into that?' "He mimicked me, 'How did you get into the napalm and the baby-killing?'

"My head spun and for a moment I thought I was going off the edge again. The images boiled up in my mind like a tape replay. Lieutenant Buckharder yelling, 'They're all VC! *Take it*, you lousy dink bastards!' The thatch roofs and bamboo walls popping with flames. Screams, the smell of burnt hair and flesh. I wasn't trained for that. I wasn't even supposed to be out there, I was trucking with a convoy that got ambushed and these guys rescued me. They were plenty short on men so they stuck an automatic rifle in my hand and told me we'd sort it out later when we got back to real life.

"I tell you, Beale, it was scary-ass times. The first day, my new squad lost two guys, the first one gut-shot from the tree line and the second blown sexless by a bouncing Betty.

"We were sweeping this clump of old bamboo huts when suddenly a 10-year-old kid lurched at me out of the shadows, waving what looked like an AK-47. I freaked and with one burst I tore him into a bloody mess.

"'Hey, go light! We're running low on ammo,' the grunt next to me yells.

"'Nice work, Nug,' Buckharder says, moving to cover me so I can clear the next hut.

"Well, Jackie-poo, my world spun right-side-up again and I saw the striped wedding party tent overhead and heard my own voice, nearly a whine as I make my case to the old guy. I tell him, 'Vietnam and Nazis? It's not the same thing.'

"But he clearly has another idea. 'I do not agree,' he says with that clipped accent of his. 'Precisely, it is one and the same. That is my point.'

"With that, he touches my shoulder, a polite gesture. 'Allow me to explain: When I was a young and carefree fellow, I thought politics was baloney. Leave me to the joys of life. Leave me alone.'

'What happened?'

'Hitler happened. Hitler didn't believe in conscientious objections. He had them hung, or drowned like rats. I saw a young man from our village who was part of the drowning. They pulled him out and left him for an example. His skin was grey marble, like one of Michelangelo's statues.'

'And so, you became a Nazi?'

'I became a soldier. I poked straw sacks with a rusty knife on the end of my old bolt-action rifle. They gave me a tin cup full of bullets and sent me to the Eastern Front. No political discussions, please. The mother country needs you. In times of war, the wise man says, *all reason is in the trumpet.*

'At first, it didn't matter. I was a young man, off to see new places. I shot over people's heads, and they ran away. I didn't want to kill another living thing, you see.

Like the young Buddhists of your Vietnam. We were
fighting the Russians, and I didn't know what they were
like.

'Then we came to this one village, a village of my
countrymen, and everything changed for me. Most of the
town was rubble, and we were fishing about for something
to eat. The Russians had been there, and now they were
pulling back. A few of us went into an old inn. It was dark
in there, and we heard a noise like a ghost:
'Ahhhhh...ahhhhhhhh...'

'My hair stood on end and I would have left, but
provisions were very low and my officer had said *Come
back with bread, a bottle of wine, some rotten cheese –
anything!*

'We discovered a man with his tongue nailed to a big,
round wooden table. He was spread-eagled on it,
stomach down, with nails in his hands and ropes around
his feet. His wife was a bundle of bloody rags in the
corner. The Russians had staked him down so he could
watch while they raped her.

'He was just the inn keeper. I didn't know him, but he
was a countryman, a simple peasant, like me. We freed
him but before anyone could stop him he snatched up one
of our pistols and killed himself. And after that I had a new
life-work: killing Russians.

'They were peasants, too; they had no concept of war
or fighting. Their officers would command and they would
rush us in human waves. I remember one place;
thousands of Russians running across an open valley.
We were a few hundred, in an old village church. This
was some months later, when I knew something about it.

I had commandeered an anti-aircraft gun with double barrels. You know? Boom!—Boom!—Boom!—Boom!'

"The old guy gestured with his fists to show the barrels fired alternately. 'They came across the bare spot of land and I shot their heads off like bowling balls.'

"And, my friend Beale, there we were, two warriors, one young and one old, still alive in a world away from all that madness; the band struck up another polka and in another moment the graceful old fart left me and soon was dipping and swaying on the dance floor.

"When he came back, I poured from the champagne bottle I'd requisitioned from one of the girls.

'Danke,' he said. 'So you don't mind drinking with an old Nazi?'

'Well... you still haven't said how you got here.'

'From Scotland.'

'Scotland?!'

'Sure. I was held prisoner-of-war there, after I was captured. Then, after the war, I met a Scottish girl and married her and we immigrated to the Great Melting Pot.'

'Is that her?' I nodded my head toward the frizzy-haired lady who, obviously winded from her dance with the wizard, waved her handkerchief from another table.

'No. I divorced the first one 13 years ago, to marry a good Yugoslavian girl I met at a dance in West Covina. Imagine. We grew up not 15 miles apart in the old country, and I meet her here in Surfboard Land!'

'Well, you seem happy.'

'I am superbly, supremely happy. I work, I dance, I laugh, I drink wine." He raised his glass, '*To life!*'

'And those Russians you shot...it never bothers you?'

'What, their heads rolling? They deserved it.'

'Deserved it?! All of them couldn't have raped that one poor woman.'

'And all the little baggy-pants in your jungles were not evil, dirty communists. You shoot; otherwise, you are a dead man.'

'How do you learn to live with that?'

He shrugged. 'You don't have to — your side picked you.'

'I could have said no.'

'Apparently the person you were back then could not find a reason or a way to do that.' He smiled faintly, saluting me with a slight raise of his glass. 'Not unlike myself with the Nazis.'

"The band started up. 'Ahh, the *Druck Polka!'* he said, and he headed for the dance floor. I wandered off and that was the last I saw of him.

"After that, I remember being outside somewhere, though I'm not sure where, and the good night rain falling on my bare head. State troopers picked me up a few days later half way to Barstow, and I ended up in the VA again. Things went fuzzy because the pills are stronger at the hospital and they'll shoot you up whenever you make them think you need it, and, you know, the months do go by.

"I'd like to say Sherry came to visit me and we got back together and things got better, but you can see she didn't and we didn't and they're not."

"I think you're looking like you're on the mend."

"Hey, don't feel sorry for me, Mister Hollywood. It's not like I'm alone here.   It's important to remember, it's never fun for anybody being the loser."

"You're not a loser, Billy."

"Yeah, I am. The winners write the history books and the losers get to polka at the parades in their ratty olive vests with the pins and colored patches."

"We didn't lose the war. Our country betrayed us."

"It doesn't matter *why* you lose, and maybe losing isn't really the point."

"What else could possibly matter?"

Bill looked angry enough to get out of bed and punch his old friend in the face. "I tell you, Jack Beale, there are nights when I stir in my sleep and that dink kid hobbles toward me again, waving his AK-47 just like he did the one time that it really counted. Only in the clear vision of my memory I can see that it's not a weapon, it's a homemade, wooden crutch, and you can give me all the lessons in the world, but I don't think I can ever learn to dance with that one."

The fierce look on Wild Bill Tilgarski's face faded to something distant and remote. He glanced around as if he was uncertain what he was doing in this place. And then his head fell back on the pillow supporting him and he stared dully ahead.

"You need anything, Billy?" Beale asked, suddenly alarmed. Still no answer, or any sign that his friend was in this world. He went to the door and stopped an orderly.

"Oh, no worry," the young man in the blue scrubs took a look for himself and then waved Beale's concern away.

"He's like that most all the time."

SOMETIMES IT'S
ALL ABOUT RELATIONSHIPS

Late-May, 1965.   One muggy spring morning about
the time the rainy season was moving in on Saigon, mail
call dropped a brick on Beale. He recognized it right away
by the special light blue color and the square shape of the
envelope, and he even had some idea what it might be
about. It was from his long-time girlfriend Grace Ann.
They had been a steady item in his undergrad days, but
*as he didn't write her very much and never talked of true
love or their future together*, she had fallen for one of his
best old-time back-home friends who had already served
his time in the military and *it was their plan to be married
and to start a family.*
  Beale did his best to shrug this news off as just
another Dear John letter, even though in one of the
compartments in his mind he had dreamed that, once he
wrote the Great American Novel and was established as a
writer, he and Grace Ann would probably, most assuredly,
maybe reconnect. He knew he hadn't been anything near

faithful or true, but for reasons he didn't fully understand that letter had him in a blue funk.

And then, a few days later, the military postal service dropped a second small bomb, this one a highly poetic note from a girl in San Francisco he'd met while at language school. Beale, who suspected what was coming, stuffed it in his fatigues blouse jacket and read it later at the White Shack. Bobbi printed her brief farewell in expressive curvy ovals that took up a lot of space:

Dear Pony-Boy Jack... I have enjoyed the ride... the wind in our hair... our walks on the beach... the guitar music by the campfire... the coffee shop in Monterey... that trip to the beautiful redwood forest... the air up there... you and I, side-by-side in our happy little tent... I thought it was us for life, you see... but love for you, Jack Beale, is the sea in a far away tree... and so in sadness, loss, and mourning I've walked alone for a long sad time until with reluctance I have unexpectedly discovered another steed to race... your memory will be hard to erase... but a poor girl has to try... I know I'll cry... but life goes on and on and on and on... Bobbi Jane Kodarski, no longer yours.

The stationary featured a drawing of a hopelessly expressive girl with enormous Betty Boop eyes staring out at the world. The sad little Boop was dressed in what looked like a training bra and panties and she sat side-saddle on a chubby pink baby unicorn. Schmaltzy as it was, for Beale it represented a little too much action on the *Adios Express*, and after a fast read he crumpled it into a ball, tossed it in the closest burn-bag and went a tad off the deep end.

And yet, as if that wasn't enough, the very next day he received another letter, this one from Patty, a tall girl with lovely smooth white skin and firm breasts that he'd briefly gotten involved with at UC, before Mavis and Janelle and somewhere between Bobbi and the continuing light rain of letters from Grace Ann. Patty typed him on a neat piece of UCLA stationary that, although it was admittedly hasty and might not be the right move in the long run she had married a nice guy named Ron that she met at a party. *Sorry, Jack, but I guess that is just how it goes sometimes. Love always, Patty.*

Maybe it was all those girls kissing him off at once, but it also might have been some other things: the My Kahn Restaurant explosion (he had dined there with a bargirl a few days before the claymores had gone off, turning the place into a bloody hell), or the *ep plastique* incident when the handlebars in a parked Schwinn blew up in the buffalo burger stand down the road from Davis Station taking out three Vietnamese peasants and the cook shortly after two guys from Beale's unit had left, or the steady drumbeat reports of torture and killings all over the countryside, the VC ramping up their campaign of intimidation to match the increasing involvement of foreign *invader-gangsters* in the war. Whatever the reasons, Beale was less able to coast along above the fray. He was feeling a disregard for the details, the little check-off list in in the routine of his daily life. This might have been obvious to anyone paying attention, but since things were very busy in his unit at that time, the only person who actually noticed anything at all was his duty supervisor.

"You let your translators go," Sergeant Hinkelby

grumbled. He'd had a grudge against Beale back at the Puzzle Palace, and it was just bad luck that here the sergeant was again, showing up like a bad penny.

Beale shrugged. "There's nothing left to translate, Sarge. We're all caught up."

"Specialist, your shift is not over for another hour."

"Sergeant, it's my unit and my call. Letting them go is good for their moral. If they don't get out of here on time, they'll never get downtown before curfew."

"You have no right to do that!"

"I believe I do."

"You're going on report, mister!"

"Sarge, you don't have a clearance and I don't report to you."

The question of *who's the boss?* was a continuing subject of friction between the lower ranking specialists – the crypto analysts, the de-coders, the ditty-boppers who transcribed Morse over the intercepts, and the linguists – and the higher ranking non-commissioned officers like Sergeant Hinkelby, who were old army but who didn't have clearances and so were by security protocol always one step removed from the actual work.

The third time it happened, Beale had already signed his men off and was ready to leave when he literally ran into Hinkelby, who came charging out of the bathroom and bumped into him.

"Where the fuck are your men, Specialist?" Hinkelby roared.

"Signed out, Sarge. Gone for the night."

"I warned you about this over and over, Beale, you got no fucking right to do that!"

One of the Beaver pilots stuck his head out of his office door. "Hinkelby, keep it down. You been drinking again, Sarge?"

"Just a few shooters at the NCO club." Hinkelby waved him off. "And mind your own damn business; I'm the duty officer here.

The pilot, a First Lieutenant, raised his eyebrows, but didn't say anything more.

"We're done for the night, Sergeant Hinkelby," Beale said, trying to push around the beefy sergeant who was standing in his way.

"The fucking war doesn't stop when you say so!"

"I know, Sarge, but our work is done, they are gone, and now I'm gone, too."

With that, Beale made a move to his left and when the sergeant took the bait and moved to block him in that direction he slid the other way around Hinkelby. Beale reached across his desk for his stovepipe hat, popped it on his head and started for the door.

The translation room was in the back of the building, and there was a long, straight corridor that led to the dark green exit door in the front. He got half way before Hinkelby shouted, "Stop! Stop right there or I'll shoot!"

Beale kept on walking.

"Stop, you stupid asshole or I'll blow your fucking head off for deserting your post!"

Beale looked back to see the First Lieutenant had come out of his office and was wrestling with Hinkelby for his pistol. Beale picked up his pace and in another moment had ducked out the door. He was shaking all over. Even though Hinkelby was drunk, not stopping in the face of a direct order was the most foolish, most stupid thing he'd ever done, and he wasn't sure exactly why he'd kept on going.

He jogged back to his barracks and changed into civvies: gym shoes, a pair of tan slacks and a soft golf shirt. He lucked onto a cyclo-van heading for the main gate and flipped a salute at the guard shack on his way out. The guards snapped to and saluted him back, certain he was an officer. All well and good, but his hands were still shaking from his encounter with Hinkelby as the cream-and-white Renault let him off at the Hong Kong Bar.

"Hey, G.I., you look lonely," a soft voice purred in his ear.

"Scotch whiskey," he said. "Not watered down."

"My name Hoa. I treat you very good-fine."

"Hoa. Blossom. You are lovely as a flower tonight, my dear." Beale bought his flower blossom a few glasses of the weak but expensive tea known as Saigon Whiskey, and she kept the scotch flowing his way.

"We go now to beat the curfew," she said. "My place, in Gia Dinh."

Beale had signed out for overnight, and so it sounded good to him.

Her place turned out to be one small room in a big warehouse subdivided into a rabbit warren of cubicles with plywood walls, none of them high enough to reach the ceiling beams high overhead. It was located next to one finger of the Saigon estuary. A relatively unsecure area, close to the edge of town. The streets were ill-lit and poorly serviced by cabs, but by then Beale wasn't paying his usual close attention. His luck held; nothing much happened except the sex and that was pretty good, so after that he and Hoa became something of an intermittent happening.

On nights when the work was light he would take off before curfew and meet her at the gritty Hong Kong. If he was running late he would take a cab and go on ahead directly to her place. Hinkelby was still hovering in the background, but the C.O. had heard about the stunt where he pulled his sidearm on one of the lingies, and so the Sergeant was muzzled at least for the short-term.

It was just another Friday after a long week decoding and grinding out translations. Beale showed up at the Hong Kong and paid for a few Saigon Whiskeys, but he didn't want to hang around until closing time. "I'll buy you five Whiskeys, if we can leave now."

She gave him her pouting little smile. "You know that not how it work. I have to stay until close up time."

"Okay, but I'm out of here. Meet you at your place."

Ba Muoi Ba is a strong beer, and Beale knocked down three or four before he left for Gia Dinh. He was lying on the bed in Hoa's cramped cubicle, dizzily watching the world stream by when there was an urgent knock on the door.

"Go away," he grunted.

"Preese. Preese. You must talk to me," the voice on the other side of the thin door pleaded in broken English.

The jerry built structure was so flimsy Beale didn't see any reason not to open the door. *Hell, anybody could punch a fist through it any time they wanted .*

He found himself gaping at a young ARVN medic fully

dressed in his carefully pressed uniform. The confusion must have been obvious on Beale's face, because the newcomer hastened to explain. "I have put on my uniform so you will believe me," he said. "You are in very great danger. The VC know you here. They do come for you soon. They now only wait for they have sent comrade to bring grenade."

"But...but...but..." Beale stammered.

"Many family live here," the young medic said. Families, many children."

Beale believed him. There was a constant wail and yammer through the thin walls, and the sound of radios was a continued tinny presence in the air.

The medic threw his arms wide; the situation was hopeless. "VC not care. They want get you. They throw grenade over wall, into here... but many people die."

Beale felt a sobering chill of fear. He didn't need any more persuading. He struggled into his shirt, pants and shoes, and was starting for the door.

"Careful," the medic warned, taking Beale's arm. "They watch for you at the front door."

"Great. What should I do?"

"Go quiet. Go fast."

He was guessing that the news he was there and a grenade was coming had somehow mysteriously travelled through the complex. Radios were snapped off and babies hushed. Beale moved as quietly as he could through the dark and deserted hallway to the big front doors and looked out on the unlit street.

His blood ran cold as he saw a half-dozen young men impatiently milling around in front of the building. He went back to Hoa's cubicle and retrieved the half empty beer bottle he'd brought with him from the Hong Kong. *Any crazy half-assed plan was better than no plan.*

He tossed the bottle down the street, and when it crashed, rushed down the stairs and pushed his way through the crowd. While they snarled angrily at him, they were physically very slight, and it looked like they were each expecting the next fellow to actually put a stop to his escape.

"*De quoc xam luoc My! Nguoi my xao!*"

Beale didn't care what they called him. A few big shoves and he was free, running down the dark street in what he hoped was the right direction. He got lucky; after three blocks he breathlessly arrived at a main cross street and caught a lone cab that was heading back downtown. He knew some friendly NCOs who had a villa on Trung Minh Giang Street near the airport, so he headed over there for the night.

The next morning, as he came in the front gate at Davis Station, the guard pulled him aside. "Everybody's talking about you, Beale. You're in the deep, deep shit."

"You missed inspection this morning and Hinkelby wants to report you AWOL."

"That's bullcrap! I signed out!"

"Well, you can't prove it, 'cause a page is missing from the sign-out book..."

As Beale approached the C.O.'s office, an orderly poked his head out the door. "Beale! Where the fuck you been? There's a call for you!"

"A call?"

"Yeah. A phone call. From stateside."

Beale hustled into the orderly room. Hinkleby was there looking red-faced and glaring through a hangover. The Captain looked troubled, but he didn't say anything, simply pointing to a phone that was off the hook on the desk next to his. Beale picked up the receiver. "Hello...?"

"Jack, *Jack!*" a female voice said, sounding tinny on the phone. "It's me, Patty!"

"Patty, why are you calling me?"

They had one of those bad connections with delays before the next person could talk. She must have misunderstood him because she repeated, "Jack, it's Patty, from UCLA." Her voice sounded pathetic.

Beale realized she was also on a speaker phone and everybody in the orderly room was listening in on their conversation. "Yes. Yes, I know. Patty from UCLA. Patty, why are you calling me like this out of the blue?"

"Jack," she said, "I realize now that I... I truly love you. I love you, Jack. I cannot live without you."

Beale didn't know what to say, but in the next second he found he was screaming into the phone, "Patty! You can't love me! You married Ron! You married him!"

"Oh Jack, Jack. That was a big mistake. You were so far away and I was so lonely..."

"No, Patty. This can't be! We can't have it this way!"

"I love you, Jack. I will always love you. Please come back to me!"

"No, no, NO! Impossible. Stick with your husband, Ron! Don't call me again, ever!"

Beale slammed down the receiver and found he was staring into one of the goofiest smiles he'd ever seen. The Captain was grinning ear-to-ear. The orderly had a shy smile on his face. Even Hinkelby had lost his habitual glare and was giving him a half-hearted *I'll get you later* look.

"I guess all lingies ain't queer, after all," Hinkelby said.

"You wanted to see me, Captain?" Beale stuttered.

"Well... I did, but I see you've already got yourself enough trouble, son." The C.O. waved toward the door with one hand. "Go on. Get the hell out of here."

HARD SELL

January 1973. Nixon's answer was a-blowin' in the wind, he wasn't going to lay a Lincoln on the American people, wasn't going to hang tough over the emancipation of Southeast Asia, a place crowded up with yellow-skinned folks who mostly couldn't speak English anyhow. Only nobody Beale knew seemed happy about his decision; half the people were angry because we were pulling out and the other half furious that it was taking so long.

Beale knew more first-hand about it than most, but he tried to stay out of the arguments, which generally turned into ugly yelling-matches. He'd been back from 'Nam since June of '65; he felt he'd done his best and had had no effect at all, and so he tried to stay disconnected, as if there was no reality there anymore.

He was still a little shaky, even though his war was a thing of the past. He'd gone, he'd seen it, he'd come back with all his limbs intact. Like a dying grunt's fairytale, barely three months after his honorable discharge, he was a copywriter for the most prestigious ad agency in Chicago, writing breakfast cereal copy for Captain Kangaroo and creating happy little chocolate villages. He hadn't lasted, of course; he had great ideas, but he didn't know how to play the game, and sometimes he got serious at the wrong things, angry at the wrong things. He moved on to L.A., and then on to Detroit to work on cars, or as they say in Motor City, *to hawk the sheet metal.*

They were shooting mostly big corporate image spots for one of Detroit's Big Three to run on Sunday afternoon NFL football games, and he was flying almost weekly from Detroit to New York or LA The agency had a long-term lease on Leslie Nielson, a golden-toned, silver-haired Canadian actor, and the car company's "Big Idea," as they say in advertising, was to come on like they were talking straight to the American people, though with a slightly superior, faintly English accent.

The outside production resource with the best reputation for shooting this sort of ad biz "true grit" was a film guy named Haskell Wexler, who ran a shop out on the West Coast. Beale got a quote, and sure enough, the price was in the ballpark and Haskell was on for the job.

Now you may have heard of Haskell, or seen his name on the credits of some pretty decent movies. He's still around, and he's a big Hollywood name with those in-the-know, but back then, he was a filmmaker about as new out of Chicago as Beale was. The difference was, Haskell had made a big wave with his quasi-documentary, "Medium Cool," a movie he'd reportedly shot with money inherited from the family shoe factory, while Beale had been disgraced from the clubby Chicago ad circles for moonlight-producing a political documentary that earned him an EMMY award and very little else. Meanwhile, "Medium Cool" had spawned a whole wave of "realistic filmmakers," and Haskell had a little stage in old Hollywood on Highland near Melrose where, in between movie assignments, he did commercials under the Dove label.

Beale heard Haskell had a lot of political liberals for friends, and that he was known to be difficult as a movie director, but he was supposed to be terrific on commercials where there was little enough of social consequence to argue about. The Sheet Metal People didn't have any problems working with him, and everybody in the office was looking forward to the shoot.

It was an early afternoon in February, a terrific Southern California winter day with blue skies and just enough of a breeze to take the cut off the hot sunlight. There was ankle-deep slush in Detroit, but Beale was in LA for at least another week. He was in a great mood as he swung his cherry red boss Mustang convertible (rented from Grants U-Drive) into Dove's small parking lot. The lot was swarming with beautiful women, dozens of All-American beauties: great legs, great faces, great bodies stuffed in tight shorts and t-shirts, and they parted in smiling flocks as he gunned the big V-8 into the vacant spot marked CLIENT. It was a cattle-call for a soft drink spot, and Beale was ecstatic. This was the *real* Hollywood! He'd been directing a few of the less expensive stand-up commercials for Ford; he'd joined the Director's Guild, and was starting to think of himself as a Hollywood-Guy-on-the-Way-Up.

But now, as he strutted past the girls in his self-appointed roll of Hollywood V.I.P., he somehow missed a step as he was reaching for the door handle to go into the Dove lobby.

He was off-balance and red-faced, and at that same moment somebody pushed open the door from inside, and he was looking squarely into the face of the ugliest woman he had ever seen... if not the very ugliest, at least, one of the most studiously homely.

Worse, it was somebody he knew, one of the girls his assistant director had hired as a go-fur on one of his little shoots. And still worse, she had to make a big scene, crying out, "Why, Jack Beale, DAR-ling!" She threw her arms wide and hugged him, planting a big kiss on his lips.

Up close like that, she didn't look any better than she had from a few feet away. Her hair was straight and unwashed, and chopped off in a ragged line somewhere down around her waist. Her teeth were chipped and stained, and her breath smelled of mentholated Kools, Maui Wowie and garlic.

Beale hated being kissed by anybody, even his ex-wife, in public. He just didn't like it, it was a hangover from when he was a kid and the aunts used to come gushing around. He staggered out of Ms. Homely's grasp, made what social remarks he could, and got inside fast.

On the other side of the door, he rubbed his sleeve across his mouth, shook his head and looked around. That wasn't real, this was. The lobby was overflowing with pretty girls. *What a job these Hollywood Moguls had!* Spirits reviving, he started down the hall. Jim, the Grey Detroit agency head writer, poked his head out of a doorway and waved a handful of typewritten pages. "Client Approval!"

Beale grinned. It looked like the final hurdle had been jumped, they had the absolute green light to do the spots.

Jim whooped joyfully, "And I've made reservations at Musso Franks for tonight!"

It was an agency ritual, when they got a big approval or finished a batch of spots, they all gathered around a noisy, crowded table at Musso & Franks for hot sourdough bread, steamed clams and many rounds of Heineken's beer.

Beale raised his hands to the imaginary god of advertising creatives and sang out happily, *"Troi, Dut, Nuoc, Oiii!"* – which loosely translated means, "Sky, Earth, Water, Everything!"

Haskell stuck his head out of one of the other offices to see what the noise was all about. He had a lean, aesthetic look and a deceptively mild manner.

"What on earth was that?" he asked.

"Vietnamese," Beale said, wondering why he had blurted that out in the first place.

Haskell perked up right away. "You speak Vietnamese?"

"Well, I used to. Forty-seven weeks at the Defense Language Institute in Monterey and a year in Saigon. I guess I learned something."

Haskell motioned to the people in the room to wait for him, and took Beale by the arm, walking a little ways down the hall to where they could talk alone. "Beautiful! What a coincidence! Look, you've got to come and see this film tonight."

Beale had only met Haskell a few days before, but the guy was an established Hollywood person, and he was flattered. *Hell, he could have steamers any time!* Still, there was something not quite right about Haskell's enthusiasm, and he held back a little.

"Okay... I guess," he said. "What kind of film?"

"Documentary on Vietnam. Beautiful footage. Shot by some Scandinavians. You'll love it."

Beale had momentary misgivings. It had been years since he'd been in Vietnam. He hadn't spoken a word of Vietnamese in all that time. "I won't be asked to translate or anything, will I?"

Haskell shook his head. "No, of course not. You've been to Vietnam, and I'd just like to get your opinion on the film. It's got a Scandinavian narration track, but we've got a translator coming to handle it." He gave Beale a conspiratorial wink. "And I want you to meet some special friends of mine... Deal?"

Beale took his extended hand. "Deal."

He pulled the boss Mustang into a parking spot on the street as close as he could get to USC, glad for once that it was just a rented car. The neighborhood didn't look too safe to him; graffiti scrawled on every available wall and a restless pack of gang kids loitering around, looking at the Mustang like it was a jeweled treasure ready for pillage. Haskell had drawn him a map to the cinema department, and he quickly hiked the few blocks to get there.

The room was small and stuffy. Ten or fifteen scruffy film students sat around a long table on which rested a projector. A white screen was set up across the room.

The kids mostly had hair down to their jackets, and beards serious as they could grow them. The preferred garment was faded army fatigues. Beale knew how hot and uncomfortable fatigues were; he hadn't worn them since the day he got out. But he could see they didn't care about that; polemics before comfort. Most wore anti-war buttons, "V for victory" symbols and neck chain pendants with the drooping triangle peace sign.

More students trickled in until the place was packed four deep back to the walls. Beale's face flushed when Haskell made up a couple things about what a great interpreter he was, how fluent in Vietnamese and what an expert on the war he was. He didn't see anybody around that looked like a European interpreter.

The film was set up on a dual projection system that Beale recognized as 16 millimeter interlock, a system that was uncommon in the advertising business, but was used by documentary filmmakers and students because 16 is cheaper than 35, and because you could show a picture around to try and sell it without taking it back to the lab for the added expense of striking a finished answer print.

Everything seemed set to go, but they were waiting for something else. Fifteen minutes more, and everybody just sat there. And then the door opened and there was a great flurry of welcomes and cheers - and in walked Tom Hayden and Jane Fonda! Jane had gone to Hanoi, been openly sympathetic to the North Vietnamese and the Viet Cong cause, and had allowed herself to be photographed in a flak helmet, peering up into the sky with a gun crew on the lookout for invading Gangster-American fighter-bombers, a picture Communist propagandists the world over had had a field day with. Tom Hayden was her husband, a famous radical himself, very influential in the anti-war movement.

Beale stared at Jane, and all he could think was she was a lot shorter than he'd imagined. When you see a star like that on the screen, they use film magic to make them bigger than life. He remembered that Allan Ladd was short too, and they'd had him walk on wooden apple boxes for his role in 'Shane.' Beale was wondering if Jane had done the same thing in Barbarella or the other sexploitation films she'd acted in back before she got social religion and began her anti-war gush.

Somebody snapped the lights off and the room full of scruffy students disappeared. The projector disappeared. Even Tom and Jane disappeared. To say it simply, Beale thought the film was *wonderful...* but he didn't love it. For the first time in seven years he was back with the people he had tried so hard to help. He could smell the rich earth of the delta, the salty smell of gunpowder, feel the muggy blasts of late-spring heat and the thick rains of the wet, taste the *pho ga* chicken soup and the salty *nuoc mam* fish sauce and the Beef Seven Ways, share again the fun and the tinny music and the bargirl laughter, hear the heavy saw of Brownings and the *PAM!!!* of the M-1s, relive the stark moments when the flares drifted down and they all wondered if the sappers would get through this time... once again the heartaches, the hopes, the agony, the screams, the horror.

The interpreter didn't show up that night, but it wouldn't have mattered, because the Scandinavian narration track was missing anyway. What they did have was a background track that was about 95 percent lip-sync Vietnamese. And the entire roomful of people turned to Beale, expecting him to tell them what was going on.

Part of him wanted to help, but it just wasn't possible. He had cauterized that part of his brain years ago, so he wouldn't go crazy. He felt numb; cased in ice. The students all wanted to know, "What are the Vietnamese saying, saying, *saying…*?" He just shook his head, his tongue frozen, brain frozen, emotions frozen.

It wasn't an empathetic time in America; there was no way those people could understand what was going on inside his head, and no way would he tell them. Pretty soon he was getting dirty looks, the students suspicious that he was CIA, a government spy dropped in their midst. Would they flog him or dip him in boiling oil if they knew he'd been in the top secret National Security Agency, or that he'd had a Top Secret Codeword classification?

It was funny, or maybe scary. Everybody Beale knew was hyper-paranoid in those times —government, the CIA, the press, the hippie activists, even Beale himself. When he'd gotten out of the service, they made him sign papers saying he would forget what had happened in those three years, "in the interest of National Security." *As if he could, as if anybody could!* Of course he didn't, and on long, sleepless nights had penned lots of it in a messy, stream-of-consciousness novel that he'd unsuccessfully peddled all over New York. After he wrote about some of that spy crap and sent the manuscripts around, he was sure HIS phone was tapped. He walked around imagining a bullet between his shoulder blades. Nuts, huh? But at the time it seemed perfectly normal, just as logical as the angry stares he was getting from these passionately foolish college know-nothings.

Beale didn't care what they thought. The Scandinavians had concentrated on the haunting beauty of Vietnam, the lushness of the countryside, the primitive grandeur of the hamlet village society, the open friendliness on the peasant faces, the political purity of the Viet Cong in the liberated zones... all contrasted with the ugliness of the Invader-Gangsters, their rusty tanks, their false and foreign ways, the unfairness of their metallic might and rain of bombs against the native integrity — and yet the native strength would win out, for right was on their side. The political slant of the film bothered Beale, but visually, the footage stunned him into submission, forced him to examine images and ideas he'd tried to forget, to look again at a people he'd tried to leave behind.

Mercifully, the picture finally flickered to an end. The lights came on, and Haskell was looking at Beale like he was a traitor, like he'd sold out his own country. Haskell turned to Tom and Jane, making his silent apologies. Beale felt he should be angry, should stand on the table and shout that they all didn't know shit, that he'd studied the whole thing, they'd stayed home chanting their comfortable little anti-war litanies while he'd actually gone to Vietnam and seen what it really was like, that the Vietnamese were good people, great people, and that they deserved to be helped, to be saved from these Viet Cong *liberators* who tortured, bullied, maimed and murdered to get their way. But he didn't. He couldn't.

He was boxed in. The entire, subtle web of propaganda half-truths, just as effective as anything he could say about a Ford or a Schlitz or a Marlboro, had him pinned like a bug on the wall. He himself was just another poisonous creature labeled *Invader-Gangster*. He saw clearly in that moment the connections extending from the first time he'd heard protestors use the term when he was a student back at UCLA, through all the hundreds of times he'd seen them in covert VC messages at the Puzzle Palace in D.C. and the White Shack in Saigon, to this little room right in the heart of one of America's greatest universities: *Invader-Gangster American. Colonialist Pig American. Nguoi My Sao, Ugly American. Number Ten, Ugly American.* Inside, where he all too infrequently thought about values like honor and giving one's word, he felt broken and crushed; but even then, as a professional, he had to tip his hat to the other side - That was great advertising!

Nobody said anything much, and when the film was finished, the meeting broke up quickly, the group thinking about the possibilities of hidden cameras and remote microphones. Feeling as isolated as a Saigon leper, Beale made his way alone through the Watts streets, walking back to the Mustang. A few young blacks were sitting on the hood talking their jive talk, but it looked like nobody had swiped anything, so he got in and drove away. Maybe he could still catch a few last steamers down at Musso & Franks.

JACK BLACKFLAG

March 1965. "Women are trouble, anyway," Harvey
Goldfine reflected, with that knowing hint of old Jewish
wisdom rising in his voice. "But when they're already
crying before you meet them – that's *real* trouble."

Goldfine and Beale had been walking along the
tarmac at the side of the Tan Son Nhut Airport runway.
Harvey was a Spec 4, and Beale was wearing his newly
minted Spec 5, the first curved stripe over the golden
eagle. They were headed from Davis Station to the White
Shack, a stout cinderblock building where Beale ran a
small section that decrypted and translated low-level Viet
Cong radio intercept messages. *Small section* summed it
up. At the time, he had Goldfine and Raymer, and that
was about it.

This was in March of 1965, the *dry time*, and so the
weather was actually pleasant, not too tepid and
sometimes even sported a little breeze to blow the smog
haze from a million Saigon charcoal burners out over the
South China Sea. It was late morning and the flapping

Hueys were long gone. Air traffic was light, just an occasional war bird lifting off to rejoin its fellows on a carrier somewhere out on the South China Sea, or taking a special order run to drop a little napalm somewhere in the jungle highlands.

Harvey and Beale were on the noon-to-eight shift. Having a little time to kill, they had stopped off at a small Army-built restaurant that featured milk shakes and massive air conditioning. The weeping woman in question was young, maybe twenty years old. She cried softly to herself during the entire time she took their order, and then stood over the shake blenders, her shoulders slumped in grief.

"On the other hand," Harvey observed, "A set of knockers the size of hers, I haven't seen this side of Honolulu."

There was no question about it. She had a large and full figure for a Vietnamese woman, who tended towards lithe and willowy. *Chinese, maybe,* Beale was thinking to himself. But Harvey was already in action.

"Co...," he said, raising his voice, "Co manh gioi, khong?" Harvey never lacked for balls, but his Vietnamese wasn't all that great. Like Beale, he was better pouring through Hoa's Viet-English dictionary than actually conversing in the field. Beale knew that, in saying hello, he'd just about maxed out his linguistic skills. But it didn't matter. The girl responded to his question with a rising wail. She rushed into a back room, leaving the blenders unattended. A glum, middle-aged *Ba* finally had to bring their soupy milkshakes.

"She's all yours, *Ong Be*," Harvey shrugged, setting

his warm shake down. "Meet you at the Shack." With that, he replaced his stovepipe hat and gave Beale a little farewell wave. In another moment he'd wandered out the door and was sauntering down the runway. Beale saw this was going to be an epic day; Goldfine was actually going to get into work before he did.

Beale sat down with his shake and brought out his twin books. He was in the heart of his Francophile phase, and he was slowly churning his way through Camus's*La Peste* with paperback copies in both English and French. He sat at one of the Formica tables and slowly moved his six inch ruler down the page. It was the season of the wet in Oran, a large French Port on the Algerian coast; rats were bleeding in the streets and things in general were starting to go sour.

After a while, the girl returned from the back room. She was daubing at her eyes with a tissue. They were large and soft eyes, and Beale, watching her out of the corner of his eye, thought her extraordinarily lovely, even in this city of beautiful women. She moved out from behind the counter and for a moment it seemed like she was going to come over to his table. She hesitated, and he smiled, hoping he was displaying encouragement rather than admiration for her breasts.

The old *Ba* behind her gave a sharp, hawking sound, something like a throat-clearing warning, but the girl ignored her. She came closer and then sat daintily across the table from Beale.

"I did not mean to scorn your friend."

"No, it's alright," Beale said.

Her tears started again, and it was a moment before

she could continue.

"Forgive to me. I am in bad luck," she said. "Bad things have come to me."

Her hand moved across the table and brushed against Beale's, just for a moment. That touch reminded Beale of the soft feathers of a small bird's wing. He wished she'd touch him like that again. Or perhaps her hand might even linger, pausing in some existentially satisfactory way with a light touch against his own.

He came back to reality with a start. There was a noise in the back room as the old *ba* talked to someone in loud disapproving tones. After a moment, an ARVN Air Force Lieutenant appeared in the doorway. He was a lightweight, probably topping the scale at 110, but his moustache, worn dapper in the Nguyen Cao Ky style, was bristling. He crossed his arms, and his lips clamped shut. The old *ba* and he both stared at Beale's table in silent disapproval.

The girl broke under the pressure and jumped up from the table. But then, wonder of wonders, that soft touch was again on Beale's arm, this time a light caress.

"We meet here tomorrow morning at this time," she whispered.

"What's your name?"

"N-Nhut," she said. "Co Nhut. And you name?"

"Jack."

"Jack," she repeated with a wan smile. She pronounced it *Zac*. *"Giac co den,"* she added. And then she gave the disapproving onlookers a dirty look and retreated behind the counter.

Beale practically sprinted to his gunmetal grey desk at

the White Shack, where he looked up the phrase in Hoa's. *Giac co den* meant "Jack Black Flag," the Vietnamese expression for *pirate*. Beale smiled, thinking that was nice in a quaint way. The afternoon of dull and boring transcriptions wore on. Beale translated SAW TWO INVADER GANGSTERS YESTERDAY. Then he broke a nasty little code and translated BONG NEED MORE RICE. And another that unraveled into SEND MORE BULLETS RIGHT AWAY. But, the truth was, his mind wasn't really on the work. His imagination was running with the Co Nhut thing. He was Jack the Pirate Lover, swooping down from his brigantine frigate to carry the pretty and vulnerable Nhut away to his love nest and shower her with doubloons and ruby necklaces and fancy silks. The low end of the spy business can get pretty dull even in a place like Saigon, and a young man has to have some way to pass the time.

The next morning, Beale showed up a half-hour early for his milkshake, and that pleased her. The old *ba* and the little ARVN flyboy were nowhere around. Beale told himself it wasn't as if he was worried about the flyboy. Americans pretty much looked down on all ARVN officers. The *Arvins*, as they were commonly called, *worked for the Americans*. Beale tried to be polite about it, but he had the same common perception as everybody else. He figured a G.I. enlisted man's stripes were worth more than all the tarnished Third World Country stars and bars in the whole damn country.

Co Nhut didn't have any problems with the flyboy not being there, either. She came over to Beale's table and sat down. Her eyes were puffy and she looked like she'd been crying all night.

"You a person of education." She indicated *La Peste* at Beale's side. "This good. I need your schoolboy help very bad."

"Anything," Beale said. "How can I help you?"

But Beale wasn't about to find out, because at that moment a group of four Vietnamese Air Force officers burst in the door, glared at their little *tete-a-tete*, and headed angrily for the back room. It was a full hand, three Lieutenants and a Captain. The Captain called angrily to Nhut, indicating with a nod that she was to follow. She jerked around like a kid caught eating a stolen candy bar, but she stood up all the same.

"Tomorrow. Here. But even more early." She hissed at Beale.

"Of course. I'll be here."

Again that delicious lingering brush of her hand on his arm. And this time, a quick kiss on his cheek. And then she was gone.

Beale's day and night were filled with lusty pirate dreams. The next morning he ran naked through the morning fog from his barracks to the shower and back again. He dressed like he was on automatic pilot, enduring a few jeering mutters from Harvey, something about the things a guy will do for a piece of ass. Having dispensed that bit of wisdom, he rolled over under his triple mosquito netting and put his extra pillow over his head.

It was still half-light and, as Beale hurried along the tarmac, a pair of Supersabers thundered down the runway, followed by an F101 and an A10. Their tails glowed as they followed one another into the low fog to do the war. Swarms of olive colored choppers rose and circled overhead and then flapped away, mostly headed north and west. An occasional dragon ship drifted in like a weary bee, returning from a night vigil of dropping flares and spraying lead around the perimeter of distant hamlets.

True to her word, Nhut was waiting inside the deserted restaurant. It was too early for a milkshake, so she got Beale a cup of coffee. They sat at the table with their heads close together and she poured out her heart to him.

Her situation was all about her brother, she said, slowing her Vietnamese down so he could catch the general drift, and repeating in halting English when she found he wasn't following. A few years ago, the unfortunate brother had died in an unlucky airplane crash. Now the United States military wanted to dig up his body, to confirm his death. But such a desecration of a grave violated all the laws of Buddha. The ghost, or *ma,* had to rest in peace. It was an outrage, a religious desecration. What sort of barbarians would violate the sacred rights of the dead?

"My English no so good," she said. "You can come to talk to them?"

"Where?" Beale asked, startled back to reality by her question. Nhut was wearing a red blouse of thin and clingy silk, and he'd been fixating on whether there was a bra under it or not. He didn't think so.

"Downtown," she said simply.

Beale thought quickly. His little lingie unit worked the noon to 8 detail, so it was doable. They agreed to meet at the main gate and catch a cab together.

This would be something new for Beale. He'd learned his little decoding games at the Puzzle Palace in Maryland, and he had a green Top Secret badge with his picture on one side and thumb print on the other, but in truth, his knowledge was highly specialized and he actually knew little about the rest of the war. Beale could tell roughly where the Viet Cong cells were nestled like cancer in this or that district or province across South Vietnam, but he wouldn't know an actual VC unless one came up and stuck a gun in his face.

Co Nhut showed up at the main gate wearing the innocent white *ao dai* and black pants of a schoolgirl. The only thing missing was the conical straw hat. If it wasn't for the knowing look in her eyes and that great body, Beale would half-expect her to throw one leg over a bike and pedal off to the academy.

"We go to my apartment first," she said simply.

Hot damn! Beale thought. They drove off towards Cho Lon in silence, Beale with visions of sugarplums dancing in his head.

The apartment was clean and bright. When he entered, a wrinkled old woman fixed him with a silent stare. *All these old ba ladies hanging around*! Nhut let out a string of some sing-song language. Not Vietnamese. Beale thought it had to be Chinese. Whatever it was, the old woman understood well enough that she'd better get out. A healthy two-year-old girl remained, staring up at him from a seat on the sofa.

"The bedroom is there," Nhut said simply, pointing to another door.

But for Beale, at least for the moment, the bloom was off his rose. He couldn't see doing it with a little kid a few feet away in the next room.

"Let's talk about what we have to do."

Nhut looked relieved, and that, in turn, took the pressure off of him. He was thinking, *You never know how a woman is going to react when you turn down a roll in the hay.*

They sat at across from each other at a small kitchen table. Beale took out a few ballpoint pens and a pad of paper.

"There is now one evil woman of America," she said.

Beale had the feeling that her problems were getting a little complex for him. He wasn't sure why yet, but he felt like he was walking ankle deep in warm and slippery butter.

"An evil American woman..." he repeated. "What did this bad woman do?"

"I already tell you," Nhut said. She sounded nettled, sorry she had confided in someone as stupid as he was. An impatient Vietnamese woman can cut you with a glance. "She want to disturb the *ma* of my brother."

Beale's loose plan of action had been a roll in the hay, hear out her story and then go to the American authorities, but here she was, spooning it out to him in little dribbles.

He shook his head impatiently. "Why don't we just go over there and talk to them now?"

That was a mistake. Her face brightened instantly. "You do this for me?"

"Sure. Where we going?"

"I show you."

She took his arm and hustled him out the door.

JAG-MACV was the legal arm of the U.S. military effort. It was on the second floor of an ordinary looking building on Le Loi Street. Beale saw right away that the people who worked there were not pleased to see them. A pimply clerk type E-3 gave him a sour look as he shoved a sign-in clipboard at him.

"What are you doing here?" the clerk asked.

"I'm with her," Beale said.

"Oh, her. You have an appointment?"

"We no need an appointment!" Co Nhut rode in on their conversation. Her voice went up a notch. The E-3 eyed her for a moment and then retreated to an office behind his desk.

After a moment, he returned with a U.S. Army Colonel in tow.

"Hello, I'm Colonel Greene," the man said. He was about 55 years old, a tall professional-looking fellow with curly gray hair.

"Spec. 5 Beale, Sir."

Beale was in civvies and unsure of the protocol, but he decided to salute, anyway. The Colonel waved off his salute. "At ease, son. How'd you get involved in this?"

Beale's heart sank. *Involved.* He wasn't just helping a native girl, he was *involved* in something.

"Well, sir, I'm stationed out at Tan Son Nhut, and –"

"Unit?"

"3rd RRU, sir. Army Security Agency."

"Clearance?"

"Top Secret Codeword."

"Badge?"

"Beale showed him the tip end of it. The Colonel held out his hand and Beale reluctantly passed his badge across. They were never supposed to wear their badges downtown, and never *never* supposed to hand them over to *anybody*. The Colonel gave the plastic square to the E-3, who immediately got on the phone, presumably to call Beale's C.O. at the 3rd.

The Colonel pointed to a chair next to a pile of ratty magazines.

"Sit over there. I'll talk to her first, and then to you."

"No," Co Nhut protested. "I want him come with me!"

"I didn't ask you, Ba Minh." The Colonel's voice had taken on a flinty quality.

He took her by the arm and led her into his office. Beale's thoughts rattled around his head like marbles in a tin can. The Colonel had called her *Ba Minh! Ba* meant she was married! *What was going on?*

Sit over there," the E-3 said disdainfully, confident Beale was going to catch a pile of *merde.*

Beale picked up a Newsweek. The kids at Michigan State were staging a protest against the war. That seemed oddly unpatriotic. Beale couldn't concentrate on the details. He flipped through the pages. Ford had a new sportster called the Mustang. Lucky Strikes meant fine tobacco. Canadian Club was smooth as velvet. From behind the paneled wood walls, Co Nhut — *Ba Minh's* voice was rising to shrill heights. Beale couldn't make out the words, but the Colonel's solid bass was right in there, counter-punching and undercutting her blow for blow.

After a time, the door opened and Nhut marched out, a study in red-faced defiance. She could have been gone five or fifteen minutes, in Beale's state of mind, it wouldn't have made any difference.

The Colonel's cheeks were also flushed an angry crimson, an unhealthy contrast to his gray locks. He nodded with a gesture that Beale took as more weary than unfriendly.

"Okay, Spec 5. Your turn."

His office was heavy with dark mahogany paneled walls, and there were volumes of maroon and green law books behind glass-paneled sliding doors. Beale stood at ease, shifting his weight from one foot to the other and back again. The Colonel sat on the edge of his big wooden desk, fiddling with the chain on Beale's TOP SECRET badge.

Ordinarily, I wouldn't say two hoots to you," the Colonel said. "But we checked out the clearance. As a top secret guy, I don't expect any of this will be news to you."

Beale felt a little shiver of anticipation. The Colonel was making the mistake people who weren't deep in the spy biz often made, that clearances were broad, when actually by their very nature they were narrow as possible, defined only by the phrase *need to know.*

"I'm going to fill you in," he continued in his weary lawyerly tone. "In return, I hope you can talk some sense into your lady friend, who represents nothing but trouble for me."

"Okay..." Beale nodded his head slowly. "What is all this stuff about her dead brother and the grave and everything?"

"Husband. It's her husband. There is no brother."

Beale blew out a deep breath and sat down. He'd just met her a few days before, and it wasn't that he loved her or anything like that. He just felt like a sucker.

"Well then, what about the evil lady from America?"

The Colonel gave him a clipped little laugh. "That's what she's calling her now? That would be Mrs. Harris, the wife of Captain Harris, U.S. Army, now officially deceased."

He saw the puzzled look growing on Beale's face. "Look, let me start further back. I have to tell you a story before any of this will make sense. Let's just say there's an unofficial program, a sort of joint venture between the U.S. Rangers and the CIA and ARVN Special Forces."

"A training program?"

"Something like that." He gave Beale an approving nod. Beale was ASA. He knew about these things. "What we are — what we *were* — doing was training special teams of expatriate North Vietnamese to go back into the North to stir things up. Blow bridges and dams. Stir up trouble."

Beale confidently nodded back at him. *He was ASA. Of course he knew all about it.*

"Right," he said.

"Our good but now dead Captain Harris was one of these gung-ho types. Probably too old to be out in the field, but that's what he wanted and he was good at it, so they let him and that's what he did."

"He trained groups of sappers."

"Yes. And, in a way, he loved his little teams of black-pajama devils. They were his boys, his men. Problem was, though it was strictly against regulations, he went along with them."

"Into North Vietnam?!"

The Colonel held up a placating hand. "Well, not exactly. They always have to be — *had* to be — strictly ARVN missions. You know, international propaganda, world opinion, the whole mess. No U.S. involvement whatsoever. Harris knew all this, but he was so damn proud of his creations, you see. He wanted to go along in the flying boxcar, pat 'em on the ass and wave bye-bye as they jumped out into the dark over the Red River Delta or wherever."

"And *did* he go?"

"Damn straight. That's what all this is about." He swung a thumb towards the door behind which Co Nhut was probably waiting with ear cupped to the heavy wood.

"This happened around Christmas, 1961. The Da Nang airport. Night. Bad weather, lots of rain. Harris finagles his way on board the plane that's supposed to wing eight of his finest northward over the DMZ and drop them with their black parachutes like little black poison seeds on enemy soil."

"Are they effective?" Beale asked, the words blurting out before he could stop himself.

The Colonel fixed Beale with a bleak look.

"Not to my knowledge. *Are they?*"

"Not that we've heard," Beale said, thinking quickly to cover his end. "Do any of them ever come back?"

"Not that I know of. But I'm saying more than I should about that." The Colonel stood and began to pace in front of Beale.

"Anyway, none of that matters anyhow, because

Harris and his merry band never get to North Vietnam. They never got anywhere. Boxcars aren't all that great in bad weather, and the damn thing slammed into an isolated hilltop north of Da Nang, killing everybody on board."

"God! Harris, too?"

The Colonel nodded wearily, taking off his wire-rimmed glasses and rubbing his eyes.

"Harris, too. Trouble is, the plane went down in a bad area. Hard to get to, and the terrible weather continued, late for monsoon season, nobody expected it. We put some heat on to go in there and get the bodies, but it had to be ARVN personnel, and they're not too keen on going out into the bush, if you've noticed."

Beale gave him another knowing nod. It was common knowledge; the Army of the Republic of South Vietnam was plagued with pacifist Buddhists who shot over the enemy's head, and Saigon Cowboys who hunkered down in their positions and never shot at anybody at all.

"Not that there was much left to find out there, anyway. The Flying Boxcar went smack into the rocky side of the hill, and there was nothing but bits and smears of bodies scattered everywhere. Very little that was big enough to be called a handful and nobody who could be recognized. We brought the bits down in body bags and gave every coffin something, though they all were a little light. You throw in a brick or something and they don't open it up and nobody ever says anything. We buried the locals here, shipped something of Harris back and that was that."

"I don't get the problem."

"Well, like I said, Captain Harris had this wife. And Mrs. Harris couldn't understand how her husband died when all he'd ever told her was that he had a safe and cushy administrative desk job. The coffin shows up back in Kansas or wherever and somebody notices it is about a hundred pounds light and there's no way to truly identify the remains. We can't tell her the actual nature of his mission. We say something vague and unsatisfactory about a training flight, but that can't be true because he's in the friggin' Army, not the Air Force. So suddenly she's not sure he's even dead. In fact, she's more and more convincing herself that he's not. And we can't prove he is. So she wants all the coffins opened."

Here the Colonel threw his hands up in the air. "Everybody else is cooperative, but your little princess out there sniffs blood."

"It's only natural," Beale said. "She has strong Buddhist feelings against-"

"Buddhist, my ass. She's a goddamn money-grubbing little bitch." The Colonel's face started to shift to its former unhealthy flush. "See, Ba Minh's husband was the pilot on that flight. His remains are spread in all those boxes, just like the rest of them. Only difference is, she won't let us dig him up."

"What are you going to do?"

"It beats the hell out of me, Spec 5. I've got to open that coffin, but I don't know how to get it done. My hands are tied. I don't have the kind of money she's talking about. And if you start paying one, you have to pay them all."

"This is all about money?"

The Colonel stared at the floor for a moment and then handed back Beale's Top Secret badge. "I'm going to have to pay her something. I just hope it's enough. Look, talk some sense into her. Tell her maybe a few thousand, that's it. You'll look like the hero, because right now, she's getting burial expenses and that's it."

And then the Colonel had his arm around Beale's shoulder and was guiding him to the door. He nodded curtly to Ba Minh. In another minute Beale and the lady were down the stairs and out on the busy street together. It was late morning and the air was already stale and hot.

She shrieked angrily for a *xe hoi taxi* and a little blue-and-cream Renault scuttled over to do her bidding. In an eye-blink they were rocketing back towards Cho Lon.

"I've got to get back to the base," Beale started hesitantly.

She reached for his arm, leaning close so that the nearest of her fantastic breasts brushed against him. "You not leave me. I need you help *now!*"

"Look, *Co* - or *Ba,* I should say -"

She burst into tears, "I must to tell you he was my brother. All people say, 'if you know I marry, you not help me!'"

"Never mind about that. Look, the Colonel said he will give you some money. But he has to see that body."

"How much money?" Her eyes glittered bright and dark through her tears.

"Some thousands, even. Maybe two or three thousand."

"Three thousand, *my kim?*" *My kim* was Vietnamese for *American money.*

"Yes, *my kim*."

Her face went dark and she spat. Her lips twisted in a scornful expression.

"It not enough!" she shouted. Her voice was so shrill the cabby in the front seat cringed like he'd been shot. She grabbed the front of Beale's striped polo shirt and started shaking him.

"You know how much wife of dead National China airman get? $25,000 *my kim*! $25,000!"

"So this isn't really about the Buddhist problems with disturbing the dead?"

"I am too a Buddhist," she shot back angrily, as if Beale was pond scum to suggest otherwise. "I also a business woman. America come over here, take advantage of Vietnam person. Take my husband, give a few hundred *my kim* a month to live on. How I to live on that? How I to buy clothes and raise my daughter?!"

By now the cab had reached her address. The cabby sat hunched over his wheel, waiting for fate to determine where next he would ride.

"I don't know! Why are you asking me?!" Beale was surprised to recognize he was shouting back at her.

"You must help me."

"I've already helped you! They will give you $3,000 *my kim*!"

"*Khong phai*," she wailed. "No, no, no. You help me more."

"What do you want me to do?!"

"Come up to apartment. We alone now. We be together. Then you write me letter to Mister President Johnson. He will give $25,000 *my kim*. Who know?

Maybe more!"

Before meeting her, Beale had always thought of himself as somewhat a fool for love. He was the kind of guy who would stand on a doorstep for hours with a bouquet of wilted daisies, just to make a point about romance. He was a *guitar, jug of red wine, and thou* type of fellow, motivated to go to great lengths to get it off and get it on. The quest was as important as the conquest, and he didn't go much deeper than that in his relationship with women. But in that moment he saw something so corrupt and vile that his lust flew out of the window, replaced by raw anger.

"You're nothing but a money-grubbing bitch!" he yelled at her in Vietnamese.

"*Sao lam*," the cabby agreed, joining the conversation. He leaned over the back of the front seat and nodded at Beale. *Very ugly, indeed!*

She looked from one of them to the other, and for a moment Beale thought she would scratch them both to death with her long red fingernails. And then she opened the door and walked haughtily away.

Beale never saw her again. Nor did he find out if Mrs. Harris actually identified for certain whether any of the remains belonged to her husband. He was sure Harris wasn't her real name. Whether or not he was a Top Secret guy, Colonel Greene was no fool.

The weeks passed and Jack Black Flag moved on, continuing his slow way through the pages of *L' Homme Revolté*. He spent the rest of his tour decoding and translating covert radio messages, and finally the glorious day came when he caught the big Pan Am jet back to 'the *world.'* The war continued its slow slide into inevitable chaos and ultimate loss.

It was actually almost thirty years later when Jack Black Flag heard again about the exploits of the ARVN black-pajama troopers who'd been inspired to fly north and take up the uncertain life of terrorists. Some brief newspaper article, buried on page two or three of the L.A.LA Times, caught his eye. There was no real news; officially, even that long after they had been kicked out of Vietnam, the U.S. was still denying these guys existed or that such adventuring had ever taken place. That was the current problem; the newspaper article was about the few aging Vietnamese lucky enough to have lived through their terrorist days. These poor guys thought maybe the people who'd trained and flown them on their missions owed them some small pension, something more than the thanks of a grateful nation.

Beale thought about the tantalizing lilt of the young woman's full breasts with a dim reverberation of his old lust, and felt a twinge of nostalgia even as he remembered once again Harvey's cynical wisdom. Of course he should have known better. But it was his first experience with that sort of thing, his waking realization of how different, like oil and water — and yet how inextricably tied — were the twin concepts of love and money.

THE BUTTER STICK QUEEN

Summer, 1977.   Beale was hanging on by a thread to his Creative Director job at a small ad agency on Sunset Boulevard when he heard that his ex-boss, the ebullient and charismatic Jimmy Gunn had collapsed and died on the UCLA tennis court after a big beefsteak lunch and a few martinis at Monty's Steak House in Westwood Village. Jimmy had lived a lusty, boisterous, dangerous life by servicing his wife and his mistress who both worked at his small agency, the wife as book keeper and the mistress as an account executive on whatever accounts Jimmy could toss her way without totally pissing off the missus.

Beale started in that little shop of mischief as a freelancer, scribbling jingles and magazine ads for the clients, but he'd performed so spot-on that the agency was using him all the time and it was costing them a small fortune. *At Piccadilly/Where the smart and the frilly/ Come out to shop every day…Be the hot dog man in your BiziBody van… America come on! Talkin' Laughin'*

Plannin'/ America come on! Talk back on a Fannon/CB radio that is... So when Jimmy's wife came to their hot new copywriter with a proposal that he sign on as the agency CD, he agreed. But one week after he'd settled into the job, Jimmy dropped by his office to rephrase the offer. *"Assistant* Creative Director, my wife meant. *Assistant* Creative Director. Me, I'm the Creative Director."

Beale tried to talk him out of it. "Come on, Jimmy, you could still be Executive CD."

"No. That's a bullshit title."

"Assistant CD, that's a bullshit title." But the new hire backed down when he saw the dangerous light in Jimmy's eyes. By that time Beale had put real cash down on a snappy little Fiat Spyder, and so he was hooked. Of course, this was a year or two before Jimmy pulled some of his financial shenanigans and got his ass fired by the main office in New York. Funny how things worked out; Jimmy moved on to an executive post at Doyle/Dane and took his honeypot with him as an assistant account exec. Jimmy's wife beat a sullen retreat to their posh home in Costa Mesa. One of the account execs took over Jimmy's spot as agency head, the agency repossessed his leased Porsche, and Beale finally got his CD stripes. That went on for a few years until the fateful day on the tennis court when the full bounty of Jimmy's life ran into its dramatically abrupt ending.

It was no real surprise that Jimmy's faithful wife and his devoted mistress both showed up at his funeral; after all, they'd been able to work things out along the way before this. The bitter *antagonistas* had formed an at least temporary truce molded out of necessity, grief, and fond memories of their newly departed stud muffin. The funeral service was a graveside affair and the cemetery was in Palos Verdes, carved into a seaward rolling sweep of green that provided a stunning ocean view for the new permanent occupant and his farewell party guests.

Beale was bothered by annoying snatches and buzzes of canned organ music as the chill wind nattered at his flaring Count Von Bismarck mustachios and tried to get in under the loose sleeves and bell bottoms of his dark blue polyester leisure suit. A thin, graying minister droned some nonsense about eternal rewards for the good people of the earth from the far side of the casket. Beale didn't know if the benediction might apply in this case; Jimmy was a cock hound of the first order, a man who did as he pleased and to Beale's knowledge had never shown any regrets.

He found himself remembering a trip he'd taken to San Francisco with his volatile boss who, over their few years together, had proven unpredictable in everything but his lust for absolute power in his small fiefdom and an unquenchable desire to bed as many women as possible, these twin attributes still in full flare right up until the excesses in his life blew out his lights.

As they boarded the commuter jet, Jimmy flashed his irresistible Irish grin and blown kisses to the stewardess and she playfully tossed bags of peanuts at him. Then he and Beale were squashed next to each other on one of those bustling, early morning flights out of LAX.

Jimmy was talking too loud, as usual, and Beale

wished he could crawl under his seat, but there was nothing he could do because Jimmy offended easily, so you had to profess continuous delight and wonder. It seems Jimmy had been attending one of those marketing seminars in Seattle when he first heard about the Butter Queen, and being lonely and after hours, he had given the phone number a try.

Jimmy's voice rose and he bubbled happily at the memory. "The Queen sounded shy and girlish on the phone, but that only heated me up, my man, and after a bit of back and forth, the child-woman agreed to come on down to my hotel. I was surprised she said yes. Knocked me over, my man! I just had time for a quick shower and there was a knock on the door and I go to answer it just wearing a towel and there they are standing together looking at me like pretty pictures in a Playboy magazine."

"They?" Beale asked.

"Yeah," Jimmy grinned. "They. The Butter Stick Queen and her mother."

"Wooh." Beale was interested, in spite of Jimmy's legendary tendency to exaggeration. "So you were busted."

"No," Jimmy's smile lit his face. "I didn't know it, but the mom was a part of the deal. And what a deal, my man! The Butter Stick Queen was a sultry hunk of youthful T&A, she wasn't that old, I guess high school age, and on top of that the mom was maybe a good looking forty. After a few preliminary *How are ya's* they each took one arm and escorted me backwards right over to the bed and got down to business."

"With butter sticks."

"I swear to you, Beale, they brought four sticks, you know, a pound of unsalted *La Creux*, and before they were through they used up every bit of it. You know, I've been everywhere and done everything, climbed Mt. Whitney and raced my own Shelby, but I've never been that high before! Pure joy, and with one pair of hands on the gas and one on the brake, they were in control for the whole ride!"

He went on with the graphic details and by the time the jet descended through the clouds over SFX most of the passengers three seats in front and behind them had an excellent visual of Jimmy's buttery adventures. Beale, in spite of his own frisking around in the tawdry offerings of war time Saigon, was embarrassed at the looks they got as he and Jimmy left the plane.

Their meeting at the wine company was an odd fiasco. The marketing manager they were to pitch was meditating in his office, not ten feet from the lobby where they waited. "He never talks on Mondays," the secretary said. "Not even to me. The Bashram Gitra will not allow it. His belief system, you know."

"But he said we were to bring the storyboards," Jimmy sputtered. "And he is working, right? I can see him, he's right *there*."

"Right. Leave the boards. We'll get back to you." She gave him the frosty, unrelenting smile executive secretaries reserve for undesirable lowlife types like admen and the guys who clean the toilets.

As they left, Beale looked over his shoulder. Bobby Vincent, Assistant VP in charge of *Tres Elegant* Pinot Noir, was sitting cross-legged on his desk. Beale had the impression the fellow was trying to levitate. He was looking in their direction, but his calm features and vacant expression said he was miles away, probably floating on a cloud out over San Francisco Bay.

Once they were back on the street, Jimmy hailed a cab.

"Maybe we can catch a plane back south," Beale suggested.

"Too late," Jimmy said. "I'll drop you off at the Fremont. We'll catch breakfast tomorrow morning, be back in L.A. before noon." Beale knew better than to argue. He spent a boring afternoon at an art movie house, had dinner in Chinatown and spent a restless night jacking off alone, and showed up at a sidewalk café at the agreed upon time.

Jimmy was there with his rumpled look and adventurer's smile, his open shirt front revealing a beige string of Hawaiian pukka beads. He was with a young woman who looked to be in her late twenties. "Beale, my man. This is Janice, the girl I told you about on the plane." Beale gave her a strained little bow and sat down and in the next second Jimmy jumped to his feet. "We've already eaten, my man. I ordered for you. Your breakfast will be here any second. I've taken care of the bill. Everything." He moved away from the table already waving down a cab. "Important meeting. Gotta run." And in another moment, he was gone.

The waiter brought Beale a plate of bacon and scrambled eggs, and a silvery pot of coffee. The girl was watching him with an indifferent attitude. She hadn't said anything. He decided she wasn't as homely as he'd thought. She had smooth, dusky skin and strong ethnic features. Italian, Portuguese, or Greek, Beale decided, the daughter of a Monterey fisherman or a shoemaker over on Market Street. Her dark stare was set under eyebrows that didn't need any darkening for definition. Her figure was on the thin side, but she looked healthy enough to heft a big patty of oleo margarine.

Beale stuttered around, trying for small talk. "You live in San Francisco?"

"No. Jimmy flew me down to see him. From Seattle." After that, nothing. Jimmy had shipped her down from Seattle, for his pleasure. More likely, for their mutual enjoyment. Beale had a pretty young wife, and he'd seen Jimmy eyeing her a time or two.

"Oh." Beale practically choked on a mouthful of eggs. He took a big gulp of coffee, burned his lips a bit.

He stabbed around at casual chatter, but she couldn't seem to put her thoughts together or maybe she wasn't interested beyond her role as a rare and exotic stimulant. He decided it would be improper to ask where her mother was and why she hadn't thought to bring her along. Maybe she travelled solo as an economy package.

He finished his breakfast in silence. He didn't have to check out until noon, but he could think of a swarm of reasons why he wasn't going to take the Butter Stick Queen back up to his room. For one thing, he deeply distrusted and resented devious Jimmy, and didn't want to be any further under his clever thumb. Then too, how could any actual demonstration of The Queen's amazing abilities ever compare to Jimmy's glowing psalm of her many ways of pleasure? Beyond all that, Beale was seriously married and didn't need any more complications in his cluttered and hard-charging life as an up-and-coming creative guru on the L.A. advertising scene. While the woman was not genuinely, absolutely homely, she was boring beyond recall. She may have been Jimmy's emollient marvel, but she wasn't doing anything for Beale. He pushed back his curled iron chair and let out a sigh he felt might pass for regret.

The girl's lip curled in disbelief. "You're turning me down?!"

"Yeah. I think so." He stood and took out his wallet.

The Butter Stick Queen shook her head. "Jimmy will kill me. He already paid for everything."

"Jimmy will never know. Look, I have to catch a plane."

"Your choice." She shrugged and glanced away as if he was already gone.

Three years and what seemed like a lifetime later, Beale stared past Jimmy's coffin at the wide oceanic panorama that, softer and more somber than a JMW Turner oil painting, retreated down the rolling slopes and away into the distance. Several miles out, a quiet fog moved in silent retreat from the effects of the mid-morning sun, inexorably gliding away like Jimmy Gunn's soul.

Beale took in Jimmy's two women standing side by side, comparing them to the Butter Queen. The trio who serviced Jimmy's needs. All three ordinary working women. All three loving or at least giving Jimmy what he demanded of them and accepting him in their lives. Beale shook his head. Why was he thinking about this stuff? Was it just the old familiar themes of sex and infidelity that ran so pervasive in the unstable and insecure ad biz? No, it was something more. It might be of some use to sort through his meandering thoughts; something was going on with him, something inside his head. What was really bothering him?

Jimmy had a talent for attracting loyalty, for gathering up people who then stuck to him like glue. The ad biz wasn't brain surgery or rocket science, but still, the people around Jimmy all seemed so commonplace. The art directors tended to be young and witless, kids minted out of art school that Jimmy would snatch up for a few nickels and could easily dump when a client flapped off to somebody else and they had to be let go. Those kids cried, loving him even as he booted them out the door. The director of research, a heavily bearded and desperately needy sapling, swayed whichever way Jimmy's wind blew. For anybody who didn't know better, you'd never think any of them were in the ad biz. They could have fit in at McDonalds or H&R Block or Ace Hardware. Beale paused as an unpleasant notion prickled his arms like the chill breeze in from the ocean. Did Jimmy, like Wordsworth's Lucy, shine because he was the only star in the sky? Or tangentially worse, did he seem to radiate with an irresistible magnetic attraction because he only allowed people around him who had nothing really special going for them? And if that was true, what did that say about his Assistant Creative Director?

NOT THIS YEAR

January, 1965. It was a week or two before Tet New Year, the biggest holiday celebration in South Vietnam. Beale was stationed at the White Shack on Tan Son Nhut Airbase, located at the west end of Saigon proper.

The White Shack was a white-washed cement cinderblock building, one story, with a burn-bags incinerator to one side surrounded by a high cyclone fence topped with razor wire. The windows were painted with thick white paint, and there was a terrible handmade poster on one wall depicting a beery G.I. talking to a bargirl. A ship was sinking in the background and the obvious slogan, "Loose Lips Sink Ships!"

Beale was on swing shift and it was late and he was hoping to get to the Hong Kong Bar and then to a villa on *Trung Minh Giang* Street that he rented with six or seven other non-coms from the 3rd RRU.

He was hustling through the usual batch of covert one-liners: *Han muon ammo* (HAN NEEDS BULLETS). *Dai nai toi sem hai nguoi my day quoc xam luoc* (TODAY I SAW TWO INVADER GANGSTER AMERICANS)Today I saw two Invader-Gangster Americans). He was about to close up shop for the night when he ran across an entire paragraph waiting to be decoded.

This was odd enough to not slip it under the pile for the lingie on duty in the morning. Covert messages are necessarily short because the senders do not want to get triangulated. Anything over one hasty sentence like "(KILLED TWO INVADER-GANGSTER AMERICAN COLONIALISTS WITH A BOUNCING BETTY)" had to be something unusual. So Beale put away his plans for the evening and pulled out his Hoa's Viet-English Dictionary. It was a simple enough primitive code. It took him nearly an hour because it was too easy. The sender had simply reversed the alphabet, plucked out the vowels and stuck them at the end.

DEAR COMRADES AND TRUE VIETMAN SYMPATHIZERS:

WE STAND UNITED IN OUR MIGHTY EFFORTS AGAINST THE COLONIALIST INVADERS AND THE IMPERIAL PIIG SOLDIERS FROM OVER THE SEA. HOWEVER, THIS YEAR, IN ACCORD WITH THE WELL-BEING OF THE UNITED PEOPLE OF VIETNAM IN THEIR HEROIC STRUGGLE AGAINST THE PUPPET GOVERNMENT AND THE LACKEY TROOPS OF THE FALSE DICTATORSHIP OF SOUTH VIETNAM, WE ARE DECLARING A TRUCE FOR THE WEEK OF THE TET FESTIVITIES, TO BEGIN THE EVENING BEFORE TET AND TO RUN A FULL SEVEN DAYS.

STAND FIRM, COMRADES. VICTORY IS ASSURED.

Well, that was thunderously big news to Beale. For nearly a decade the Viet Cong had been threatening to launch a huge victory assault on the national holiday. Here it was 1965 with a few days left until Tet and he knew there would be no Tet uprising this year!

Beale's mind raced with the implications: American and ARVN manpower could be shifted; outposts could be resupplied with less fear of enemy activity, maybe even lives saved!

Beale typed his translation with trembling fingers and rubber stamped the special TOP SECRET CODEWORD on the top in red. He ripped the paper out of the typewriter and ran down the hallway looking for the officer on duty.

But he was late and the lieutenant had left the White Shack in the hands of the sergeant on duty.

"I've got a hot one to go to the States!" Beale told him.

The sergeant gave Beale a baleful glare. They had had words before. "Yeah, and I got a mother in Milwaukee who wanted me to be a priest," he said, picking his teeth as he looked up at Beale from the remains of a buffalo burger on his desk.

"No, Sarge, honest! This is special!" Beale had stamped his translation with the highest priority codeword. That meant it was supposed to go out through a system that coded it and jumped it from ship to ship across the Pacific and through special land line circuits across the States directly back to the Puzzle Palace at Fort Meade in Maryland. It could be back at Meade, half way around the world, in minutes, a very big deal back in 1965.

Could be, but wouldn't be. Beale's translation was

dumped in a sack with the rest of the one-liners. It would be back at Meade in three days. Swing was over and Beale was an hour or so into the night shift. He had missed the bus back to barracks, so he decided to hoof it, a little less than a mile down the runway to his waiting bunk underneath the double layers of mosquito nets.

He was scuffing his feet, looking down as he walked along the tarmac, disgusted with life in general and the army ways in particular. *How the hell did they expect us to win the war?!*

He glanced up and was stunned to see a glorious but entirely alien night sky. It was a clear late-winter night, and the Southern Cross hung gloriously above the horizon. He would never forget that night, the night he realized they weren't going to win the war.

A few months later, when the White Snake came around with his re-up package loaded with bennies, he quietly but firmly turned his promotion down.

"But these are hard stripes!" the officer yelled, as if Beale didn't understand the Army.

Over the decades since, he sometimes wondered if anybody who cared was on duty three years later, the night the comrades called for the bloody uprising that turned the tide of American sentiment against the war and changed the course of history.

TRUE PATRIOT

December 1968.   Beale ended up back in Chicago where he worked for a blue-chip ad agency famous for home-spun mid-American humor, good old-fashioned patriotism and down-to-earth long-running campaigns for products like peanut butter, beer and fountain pens.

He made an arresting figure striding through the swirling snow flurries along busy Randolph Street, puffing great clouds of steam and wearing Peter Max t-shirts and tattered blue jeans under his olive drab army greatcoat, his feet freezing in mismatched cotton socks and thin rubber-soled sneakers.

After 'Nam, he couldn't seem to get cold enough; he was always unbuttoned, and his long blood-red woolen scarf (knitted by an old girlfriend, now married to a buddy who'd stayed behind) and the corners of his coat and his matted, sun-bleached hair flew angrily in the raw winter winds pouring off the iced-over edges of Lake Michigan.

Two cops sitting in their squad car were parked at the curb in front of the Prudential Building.

"Hey, look at that weirdo. Want to toss him?"

The second cop waved with his thermos. "You toss him, Ron. Too cold out there to be fucking around."

Ron put on his checkered Chicago cop hat and got out of the car. "Hey, *you!*" he shouted. "What you think you're up to?"

Beale walked on as if he didn't hear him. In the next second the cop had him in an arm lock and slammed his head against the top of the squad car.

"What, don't you understand English, Hippy-Dippy Asshole?"

Beale didn't say anything, and the cop let him go, thinking maybe he'd knocked the stupid beatnik out. But in the next second his collar turned and glared at him, fists clenched, still saying nothing.

His partner, shaken by the loud sound of Ron's victim slammed against the car, hurried from the driver's seat. Ron had been on the pad a time or two for use of excessive force.

"Hey, what's happening?"

"This asshole won't talk!"

"Well, that's not a crime, Ron." He turned to the gaunt figure in front of him. Blood was running from a cut over his eye and his cheek looked bruised. "You got some I.D., buddy?"

Beale dug in his pocket and shoved his wallet at the officer, who took a step back before he took it. You never knew what a weirdo was going to do.

"Jack Beale. Okay, Jack Beale, what's going on with you?"

Still, Beale refused to talk, but the expression on his face said he was ready to kill.

"I hate it when they wear the flag sewed on their ass. Where did you get that Army coat, you hippy freak?"

"In the Army," Beale said through clenched teeth.

They locked him in the back seat and called it in. After five minutes, the doors unlocked and Officer Ron said, "Get out of here, Hippy-Dippy!"

Beale stormed out of the car and resumed his march down Randolph Street, not looking back, as if they no longer existed in his life.

"Wooh, there goes a strange one," Ron said.

"You have to be a little more careful, pal," his partner warned. "He looked like he wanted to gut you like a fish."

"That mad, huh?"

"Not really mad..." The officer thought about it for a moment. "More like he was in another place."

He could be weird. That morning when Chris, his boss's secretary came to call him to a creative meeting he grinned at her and pointed to the cheap rug he'd thumbtacked to the back wall of his cluttered cubicle.

"Know what that is, Chris?"

"No, I don't," she frowned. She didn't like to talk to him. He didn't have the right attitude.

"It's a Montagnard marriage blanket."

"Who are the Mont-ag... ahh, forget it."

"Aboriginal hill people in Vietnam. If I can wrap it around us, we're married."

She gave him a smug look. "You wouldn't dare!"

He didn't like Chris. The Creative Director's smug and pudgy-legged little secretary had made it a mission to come spying on what he was up to. In one motion he jerked the rug from the wall and lurched around the desk after her.

Her eyes widened and she retreated down the hall. She quickened her pace when she saw he was still coming after her, holding his stupid rug out like a bull fighter.

She was chubby and it was difficult trying to run and at the same time hold her tight mini-skirt down over her butt so her panties didn't show. He could have caught her in a flash, but he grunted like a lusting savage and stayed just behind her as she ran screaming down the hall, her fat, mini-skirted thighs flapping, her head-banded hippie *au natural* look draining to panic under the florescent overheads. Once he had all the art directors and copywriters laughing as they poked their heads out of their own cubicles, he folded his rug and headed back to his office. He knew he still had a few minutes to calm down before the creative meeting.

The irony was, his robe really was an ancient marriage blanket, a symbol so remote and distant from the Midwestern American way of life that the average citizen of the Windy City couldn't be expected to understand what that was about.

Same-same, that was the way it was whenever he started talking about 'Nam. His voice would rise, the tic in his right eye starting, and his nervous hands gesturing, and the Chicago-present would fall away from him as the ghosts from his past returned.

"Friend, will you give for me just two piasters?" The leper's bad eye hung from its socket and the whitish, rotten stumps of his elbows and knees peeked through rag wrappings, and yet he grinned up from his homemade skateboard with a fierce, indomitable cheerfulness.

Beale had scribbled images like that which at odd moments had formed in his unconscious mind, and had push-pinned them everywhere on his walls. Bits of paper, backs of envelopes, scraps of newspaper, old pastel fliers filled on the blank back side with his cramped, impatient hand, piled pell-mell in his desk drawers, crumpled in his pockets, paper-clipped in rumpled stacks, tossed in shoeboxes or in the major mess that his old Army footlocker had become. He couldn't force himself to go back in there and pull it all together into a novel, though he'd tried a dozen times.

He tried to keep quiet, but everybody he met had an opinion, hawk or dove, and he found both positions naive and stupid. And everybody asked him. After all, he was a vet – he'd been there, for Christ's sake, what did he think? So they'd get him going, but everything he talked about from that far away world sounded so alien, so different from the short, disastrous news-bite horrors that bled out of the television each evening that they couldn't relate to what he was saying.

And all the while, the mounds of chicken-scratched images were building in his pockets, his shoeboxes and his mind.

"Friend, FRIEND! You like suckie-suckie? Hundred P Alley just over there! Gap Tooth Annie clean you clock plenty good big time!" The street kids were half-naked and filthy, and swore like Marines in marvelous bursts of pidgin French-English.

"But what are they like?" the people at the agency wanted to know.

"Well, I found the peasants were an incredible blend of innocence and corruption, and yet they could be good, loyal friends, and funny, too."

Beale could see the look of skepticism fade to one of disbelief. "Naw, come on. We're talking stupid Stone Age Buddhists here, right? Come on, no more crap, give me the real story."

And Beale would retreat into his memories.

"Friend, do you want eat rice-with-crab?" The club-footed cripple laughed and shoved a begging bowl a few inches from his face, a cheap wooden bowl crawling with maggots. A few minutes later the cripple was hobbling on his crutches, a lot faster than Beale would have thought possible, with a pair of White Mouse cops in hot pursuit.

At lunchtime Beale was heading out to a sound recording studio to hear his new 'When the sun comes up in the morning' breakfast cereal jingle.

The receptionist on the thirteenth floor stopped him as he was sweeping past. "Hey, Jack, I hear you were in Saigon."

"Yeah, right," he said, stopping at her desk with a

vague and distracted look on his face. "What are you putting on your fingernails?"

"Love Pink," she grinned, "What do the girls wear in Saigon?"

"Probably Love Pink."

"Naah. I mean, stop kidding around."

"No. They are the same as girls here."

She shook her head, wondering how that could be. They had to be different with their cults and brothels and incense and everything. She wanted to ask him more, but the phone rang and she had to take that. By the time she turned back to him, he was gone.

She teased him with a lock of her long black hair, brushing it gently against his cheek. "I new in from the countryside, G.I. – you want buy for me one Saigon Whiskey?" She was young and slim and mysterious, and he had no way of knowing in two days his friend would see the white-gray of her brains blown in his face over a bowl of pho ga.

After the music session, Beale and a few of the others ended up at the Hong Fu Chinese restaurant on Michigan Avenue.

"Sooooo," the art director on the "Sun Up" campaign asked him. "What was it really like over there? Not that I'm signing up for a tour, or anything like that."

"Well, the people are like here, just trying to do their lives."

"Hey, I see the nightly news on TV. Fuckin' savages, man, cut a little girl's hand off for going to government school."

Beale's face reddened. "We had our chance to rescue a decent people and give them their freedom, and we're screwing it up!"

"Oh," the art director said, burying his head in his menu. "Are the egg rolls any good here?"

"Here's your dragon-dolly, Little Sweetbread, do you want to go to bed?" Tuy was a few months shy of 16, but none of the troopers cared, least of all his friend Charley... his friend Charley... his friend Charley...

Once he'd thought about Charley, whose spirit had left his tortured body somewhere on a hillside in Tay Ninh province near the Cambodian border, the rest of his day would be ruined.

Still, no question about it, Beale was the resident mad genius. When he got the idea to do the new Apple Cereal logo in finger-painting, he rented a stop-frame Boleaux and some lights and spent the night on the thirteenth floor, breaking into the candy machine sometime after midnight, and painting with his fingers on a glass partition in the reception area, spilling pigment on the floor that was never really cleaned up until they replaced the carpeting. That little mess cost over five grand, but the new logo glowed like stained glass, it was almost a religious experience if you were into new product introductions, and all was very well.

Instead of story-boarding his Sunrise Cereal commercial he went out to a near-north side marina and filmed it with a hand-wound 16 millimeter Bole and some wannabe local actors, infuriating a department of talented art directors who saw a radical loner cutting the Gordian knot they depended on for their big paychecks, and similarly outraging the agency producers who saw their first class trips to LA and New York City shrinking into cab rides to the local labs to pick up rolls of processed film. But they saved 30 big ones on that job; no small peanuts in those days, so he got away with it.

The average perky secretary on the prowl for Mister Right left him strictly alone, and it wasn't just the weird marrying robe. They decided he was a hot flash, this week's boy-wonder, definitely not the kind of guy you could count on for two kids, a station wagon, a home with a big front lawn in Lake Forest and a bushy dog named Flubster. If they needed any further proof, all they had to do was look at his friends. He hung around with actor-types and mod painters and artsy-fartsy filmmakers and flaming faggots and an assorted bag of weed-smoking loser-hippies – undependable people who had the wrong demographics, which meant they weren't important in the advertising world because they didn't buy things.

He had intense, piercing eyes, old for his thirty years, and a strange way of looking first at, then through and then beyond you, a mannerism that made him seem to drift inexorably from the person being eyed to the imponderables of the universe, a stare that intimidated all but the most self-assured who crossed what he called the DMZ (the so called demilitarized zone between North and South Vietnam) and entered his office. He had two laughs: the genuine, amazed and innocent laugh of a boy, which was heard rarely at the agency, and a sardonic, brittle-rimmed chuckle that made people uncomfortable.

And because he was good and he really didn't care about anything, he hit a hot streak that carried him through for quite some time.

He had his problems, but that happens a lot in the ad business. There were the erratic hours, the unexplained absences, sudden fits of rage, shouting matches with account types and clients, hints of alcohol and dope binges, and arrests for various odd things.

They patched him up, of course, the same way they bailed him out of his troubles with the police. By the first time he'd gone off the deep end he'd already invented the six million dollar Chocolate Village campaign and the classic stop-framed Pop-Ups commercial, which convinced a generation of Americans that dry slabs of frosting-coated cardboard wheat with a little strawberry jam in between was the fast and tasty mod way to greet the day, and nobody else could write the Fooper Bear Adventures that explained to kids why their parents had to continue buying the soup with pasta bits shaped like little bear paws.

So, after the cleaning ladies found him with his multi-colored blanket around his shoulders staring at a blank television screen at three in the morning, the head of the agency sent him to a special lakeside retreat in northern Wisconsin for a couple of months, where he was ostensibly location scouting for a pool of menthol cigarette commercials. It was an exclusive and well-kept place in the green forested pot-and-kettle hill-and-lake country. There were miles of fenced-off woods to roam, bubbling brooks to contemplate, and puffy white clouds to fall asleep under.

That's how they'd put him back together. They'd wind him up and out would come pouring Motown-singing plaster planets, cereal-stealing cartoon dogs, box-top blimps and talking chocolate – the wildest batch of crazy nonsense ever used to sell a product.

Sweet Ecstasy, the bar that begs to be bit! The candy mill in Chocolate Town makes candy bars so golden brown! Kids, Fooper Bear and his pal Old Man Vita-Mine, the good-health prospector, say, "Now's the time to get out your Fooper-Dooper spoons!" "When the sun comes up in the morning, time for Sunrise Cereal!"

It was pure gold. They called it 'creativity' and excused him for caring too much. His every excess proved their point; nobody gave, nobody cared about the agency's clients, their products and the American way like Beale did.

LUCK

April 2012   Beale was waiting for his old Army
buddy, Bill Tilgarski, at his favorite Starbucks on Little
Santa Monica Street across from an agency known for
repping superstars and big name producers and directors.
Beale had never hit it big enough to where those
schmucks had showed any interest in repping him, but
you never knew who you were going to bump into, and
maybe Wild Bill would get a kick out of it.

Bill showed up on a maroon Harley and swept in with
a flourish, crackling with energy. His light yellow hair was
nearly white now, but he still had a big mane and looked
every bit the Old Lion King.

Beale couldn't hide his surprise. "My God, man, you
look your old self!"

"Right!" Bill grinned. "You mean my old, old self back
before I became a deadhead!"

"Yeah. That is what I mean. Last time I saw you, was
at the V.A. hospital down the street from here…"

"I know. And I wasn't in such great shape."

Beale pounded him on the back and they grabbed a couple of lattes and scones and commandeered a table in the back.

"Billy-boy, what are you doing in town, anyway?"

"Headed for Fiji to look at some beachfront property. I love beachfront, but there isn't so much available in the States any more. Where you live these days?"

"Annapolis. Just up the road from the old Puzzle Palace."

Beale shook his head, trying to match this Bill Tilgarski with the pathetic vet he remembered from years past, but Bill just laughed and clapped him on the shoulder. "Hey, guy, that's all behind me now. I got what I deserved, I paid the price, I slogged through the mud, I saw the light, I self healed, and here I am!"

At the hyper-sensitive Puzzle Palace, Wild Bill's impatience with Army ways had cost him his clearance and he'd ended up with a dangerous gig in South Vietnam, driving a truck in convoys out in the bush. Those times being what they were, he had more than his share of blood and horror from the delta to the Z. Somehow he'd survived to muster out of the Army with an honorable discharge, but by then he found himself out of sync with civilian life as well, and his decades-long downward spiral had begun.

"But look at you. Here you are!"

"Yeah, good as new, just fifty years older."

"What happened?"

"Nobody really knows. A couple of hours after 9/11 I woke up to see myself staring at the television screen. That was the way I was back then, just set me in front of a

TV and I would watch whatever was on. Except at that time, what was happening was a lot of smoke and ordinary people running through the streets and jumping off the twin towers as they fell and I said to myself, *By God, the sons-of-bitches have finally made it over to the States!*

"When the day orderly saw what I was watching, he tried to switch over to Jeopardy, but I told him to get the fuck out of there, and he did.

"A few days after that, I disappeared myself from the VA hospital. They reported me missing, but nobody was concerned as I was always running away. The docs assured everybody I would come back for the meds.

"But I guess I fooled them. I went cold turkey on a Greyhound bus and two nuns and a schoolteacher nursed me back to health somewhere between D.C. and the Mississippi River. After some weeks on the bus I decided to go back to Annapolis and live in an old summer cottage on an inlet south of the Naval Academy that my dad had left me.

"What a mess! The place hadn't been lived in for a decade, but I cleaned it up and it was okay. There was some property, so I sold it except for an acre. I started day trading on my dad's old computer, and the rest was history."

Bill grinned across the table at me. "But how about you, old friend? Still the sho-biz whiz?"

"Nah. Never was that. Just thumping along, day to day. Directing commercials, mostly."

"Big time!" Bill's smile widened.

"No. Honest." Beale pointed out the window to a big

chrome-and-glass building where a steady stream of people were coming and going. "Over there, that's where the Hollywood success stories are made. They're not interested in a little guy like me."

"But you're in the Director's Guild."

"Yeah, sure." Beale shrugged, wishing the subject would go away. "Along with sixty-seven hundred other directors."

"Wooh, look at that hot chick!" Wild Bill pointed enthusiastically across the street to where a slim, leggy Eurasian girl was hurrying into the building. "Kind of reminds me of that gal you were dating in 'Nam."

The expression on Beale's face stiffened. "No, I don't think so."

"Yeah, she does. Therese, right? Her name was Therese."

Beale reluctantly admitted it was, or at least had been, he had no way of knowing if she was even still alive.

"Remember, I came down from the highlands and you fixed me up with her friend."

"Yeah. I guess I do remember that. We went to a movie at the Arcade Edan."

"Those were some fine chicks, man! Not your usual bargirl hooker whore types. 'Hey, G.I., you buy me perfume from the PX.'"

By now Beale really wished Bill would change the subject, and he wasn't sure why. "I don't know what became of Therese," he said, "and I don't care, not really."

Bill nodded agreeably. "Yeah, long time ago in a country far, far away, right?"

That was one thing about Wild Bill Tilgarski, he'd

always been a great listener, and so, after a moment thinking back to those times, Beale found himself telling a story he hadn't thought about in a long time.

"Billy, it's not like it was some big deal or anything. Remember how young we were back then. I don't know about you, but I didn't want to be serious or committed to anybody."

"Well sure, me neither. And look where that got us... You have any kids?"

"Yeah, I have a daughter somewhere who hates me just like her bitch mom taught her to do."

"I never knew you were married."

"Three times. Not anymore. And you?"

"Divorced, two kids, they don't even know I'm alive. But back to happier times..."

"Yeah, our vacation in the tropics."

"I thought you would say *Fuck the Army* and marry sweet Therese."

"It wasn't like that for me. Back then, it was all about survival — you know, how to get through with my skin in one piece. Bill, I know you had it lots rougher than me, but to tell the truth, I didn't think I was going to make it, either. To a superstitious person, the warning signs were everywhere."

"Go on! You were superstitious?"

"Billy, if you scratch any man of science in the right place he'll bleed voodoo mumbo all over you. Try it on yourself if you don't believe it — stay up all night in your family cemetery or at some roadside spot where somebody you knew died a violent death."

"Amen to that, bro. I never go see my parent's grave.

I think they'll ooze right on out of there for all the bad I've done."

"When I first landed in-country in June of 1964, my boss, Sergeant John 'Red Dog' Moore, warned me against going downtown Saigon too often, or with the wrong crowd. I remember the first time we rode over to the third 3rd RRU in his Jeep. He took both hands off the wheel, waving them in the air, and he shouted, 'I'm responsible for them! But noooo, them frickin' college grad-u-ate asshole nugs don't listen to nobody! And they keep dying on me! And I say to God Almighty, it is not my fault!'"

"Well, Billy, I didn't think any nugs had died, but as I was a nug myself, I wasn't sure about it. I tried to change the subject, but Red Dog didn't want to talk about the weather. He wanted to tell me about our C.O., a story that was guaranteed to convince me of the dangers of downtown Saigon.

"'Listen up, nug,' Red Dog shouted over the noisy Jeep and the traffic, 'this here C.O. was a wise and prudent family man, a responsible and worthy officer who only ventured into sin city once a month to pick up the new issue Vietnamese postage stamps for his kids. It was his custom to take a Navy bus called 'The Grey Snail' to the Main PX and then hire a pedi-cyclo to take him a few blocks over to the big post office, the *nha buu dien,* to select his stamps. The Grey Snail was a school bus with heavy chicken wire bolted over all the windows. It was generally considered safe from terrorist attacks.

"'Well, one time on his monthly trek, the C.O. gets off the snail, but on the way over to Hai Ba Trung Street to pick up his stamps, his wiry old cyclo-boy fellow informs him he's got to stop for *thuoc la* Basto, that is, he has the nicotine urge so bad he has to pause right then and there to buy a pack of those god-awful Basto Reds.   Reds smoke like burning dog turds, and Blues aren't much better, but they are both cheap as sex and about as much as a cyclo-boy can afford.

"'Anyway, the skinny old cyclo-boy disappears around the corner and, after a minute or two, the C.O. gets suspicious and follows after him. The cyclo-boy is nowhere to be found but, as the Captain rounds the corner, the seat of the cyclo from which he has recently vacated his plump Western *derrier* erupts in a violent ball of flame. Somebody had rigged a crude timing device to a few sticks of dynamite. Rumor was, blowing up a U.S. officer was worth 5,000 piasters, and that translated to a couple hundred bucks *my kim* (American) at the time. And our trusty C.O. never went back to town again!

"Billy, I was sure Red Dog told me that story just to scare me. But he needn't have bothered; I was already frightened enough. I'd just gotten off the jet, as they say, and was expecting a hail of bullets from any direction."

"What ever happened to him?"

Beale nodded and held up two fingers to the Starbucks waitress, who nodded and hurried off.

"Things have a funny way of playing out. A week or two after telling me how dangerous things were in downtown Saigon, Red Dog drove his Jeep a few blocks over to the airport restaurant and, as luck would have it, he walked in to order a burger and fries just as a 40 kilo package of *ep plastique* detonated. Red Dog was high-

163

speeded to Saigon General and then, as soon as he stabilized, was to be flown to a hospital on Clark AFB in the PI.

"They were always short of blood at Saigon General and, as I have the much-desired O neg, I went down there to let them siphon off a pint and a half, the amount they usually drain out of the young and the healthy in a war zone. After that, I took the slow and clanking elevator up to see Red Dog. He had crossed eyes and chunks torn out of his skin on about half his upper body. He was doped to the gills, but he managed to tell me I had to go over to the Bristol Bar and let his girlfriend in on what had happened to him."

"Didn't seem to have stopped you any." Bill stood and insisted on paying for the second round of lattes.

"Well, I was crazy back then. I had developed my own theory about luck. It was all about space and time. Bad luck was no more than occupying the wrong space at the wrong time. Good luck, of course, was the opposite of bad luck, and good luck only settled on the shoulders of those who stuck it out there and refused to cringe."

"Luck. You went to downtown Saigon because you felt lucky."

"Yeah. I thought I had it all figured out. Luck was a wave you rode, like a surfer. It was a lane on the highway of life. Luck and her twin sister Confidence were like powerful currents in the river."

"Highly poetic, my friend."

"Right. Beale the poet. All you had to do was stay in the center of the current, and everything would be okay. I thought it was my own theory, I think a lot of young people think like that. The young and the foolish."

Wild Bill's smart phone was beeping, but he clicked it off without even bothering to look who it was. "Sooo… what does this have to do with the lovely Therese?"

"Patience, oh ye of little faith. I'm getting to that. The truth was, as the months were ticking by, my luck theory was taking somewhat of a toll. That was about the time I developed a nervous tick in my right eye and a set of hands that sometimes shook so badly that I had to sit on them. Scotch, I found, was good for calming both these symptoms."

Bill nodded. "I know the feeling. But you didn't stop going downtown."

"No, I didn't. The lesson I took from Red Dog was that I couldn't spend my time hiding out on Tan Son Nhut Airbase, eating mess food at the 3rd and working my tour away over at the heavily refrigerated White Shack decoding low-level crypto. Hell, I could have done that back at the Puzzle Palace in Maryland. If the bullet or the mortar or the explosives were going to get me, they could just as easily take me in my bunk or while floating over the countryside in one of the radio receptive Beavers or walking along the runway through the driving rain between the White Shack and Davis Station."

"So you went the other way, flew into the storm, as it were."

"Yes. I became the ultimate culture junkie. Every second when I wasn't working, I went downtown. I went alone, just me and my sharp-lens little 35mm Bolsley Jubilee. I would throw on a set of casual civvies and went off-base. I hung out at the racetrack, the zoo, the old

Saigon market, the fortune-teller's block and a dozen other places where Americans just didn't go."

"No whore hopping? Doesn't sound like you."

"Well, no. I went to the bars and the nightclubs and to the Chez Renez, everybody's favorite whorehouse in Da Cau, but that was just the shallow end of the pool. I had volunteered for 'Nam and lucked into an assignment in Saigon. I was going to see it all!"

"Less than 20,000 G.I.'s in-country at that time."

"Yeah. This was before our build-up. The city wasn't full of Americans. I worked swing shift, but my mornings were free. I took a job at the Hoi Viet My, teaching English to Vietnamese kids. I lucked into a second job, as an announcer at *Nha Vo Tuyen Truyen Thanh* VTVN (the real native Radio Saigon), and soon had my own show, The Happy Jack Platter Shop. I went in with Crazy Jack Waer and a couple of other NCO's from the 3rd to rent a villa over on Truong Minh Giang Street. In short, I so rarely slept in my bunk at Davis Station that I had to pay someone to keep the sheets tight for inspections."

"Wooh. Jack Beale goes native."

"Yeah. I did. And the months passed and my sorry-assed Vietnamese became almost coherent, the bad rainy season came and went, and my luck seemed to hold and hold and hold. I walked out of the Anna bar and it blew up behind me, four troopers down. I was heading towards the Bank of Tokyo to cash a check from the Hoi Viet My, hailing a cab and no more than two minutes away, when the U.S. Embassy across the street from the bank was hit with an explosion from a small car packed with *ep plastique*.

"Lucky man."

"And I was decoding and translating low-level covert VC intercept the night the terrorists set off two claymore mines on the My Canh floating restaurant. I'd been there two days before. Anybody could see it, if they cared to look; I was in the heart of my luck, cruising towards short time and looking forward to that big Pan Am ride that would take me back to The World."

"And…?" Wild Bill grinned like he knew what came next.

"Uh huh. And then I met Therese."

"I remember her. Beautiful woman."

"Yeah," Beale's face took on a sad expression. "Too good for me, right?"

"Naw, I didn't say that."

"She was only eighteen. She worked at the Maison Blanch, a dress shop in the Arcade Edan. Her family was Catholic, and she spoke pretty good English, though with a French accent. Her mother owned the dress shop, and was not friendly."

"And you fell for the daughter like a ton of bricks."

"Don't be silly," Beale said, the irritation evident in his voice. But after that he was silent. When he finally spoke, it was with a more reflective tone. "I did like her, though, and we started seeing a bit of each other."

"Ahah!" Bill couldn't resist the jab.

"No, no, no, nothing like that. We weren't, like, intimate or anything. Christ, imagine how that would have screwed everything up! Think about it, a real girl who didn't want you to buy her another Saigon Whiskey or some Toni hair spray."

"Sounds like you were getting a little serious."

"Well, after I met Therese, my random jaunts through the streets of Saigon tended to end up at the Arcade. I took a look in the mirror and decided I didn't like what I saw, so I tried to change my ways. I stopped bringing stray bargirls over to my room in the villa."

"Wooh, that's a big step."

"I know," Beale nodded. "I drank less scotch and bought a new sports coat from an East Indian tailor over on Hai Ba Trung Street."

"I heard about that guy. He advertised genuine Hong Kong wool — just bring him any photo of a suit or jacket from Playboy and he'd make it up in five working days."

"That's the guy. Well, as the weeks went by, Therese told me about her brothers, her vacations to Da Lat and Cap St. Jacques, her relatives in Paris. She talked about her schooling, and how she would one day have the biggest wedding in Saigon. She had wide and beautiful eyes. I liked the way she looked when she talked about her dream. She would float down the aisle of the Saigon Cathedral in her white gown. God, I remember those full rich lips, pouting just a little bit as she looked me over; *I dare you*, written all over her."

"It's starting to look like you're drifting into dangerous waters here, Specialist Fifth Class Beale."

"Maybe, but back then I didn't realize I was drifting into dangerous waters. It didn't matter. Not the war, the terrorist bombs, my TOP SECRET CODEWORD job, the pro-war and anti-war mess building back home. Nothing mattered except those wide dark eyes and her sweet lips."

"Christ, you had it bad, man."

"Maybe," Beale said again, this time with a shrug. "But then something happened that changed everything: one Saturday morning in April of the year 1965, I was walking up Tu Do Street, making my way slowly from the river towards the Arcade. I was carrying a photograph of me, specially framed, something Therese had asked for. She didn't get off for lunch until noon, and that day I was early and in no particular hurry.

"I know you weren't stationed in Saigon, Bill, but this was the street that offered the most elegant shops. There was still a French presence: Air France, Renault, Chez Brodard's fine clothing and dress shops featuring elegant European styles.

"I remember I had stopped in front of a fine leather goods store to study some wallets made of ostrich and elephant skin when I heard some sort of backfire followed by a *chink* in the glass over my head.

"I thought that noise was out of place; strangely interruptive and brittle, just above me and a bit to my right.

"I turned around and found myself staring at a young man on a motor-bicycle."

"Oh, shit," Bill said.

"You got that right. He was sitting on one of those little black Solex bikes, parked just next to the curb, and he was pointing a revolver at me. I looked above me. Sure enough, there was a starred hole in the plate glass window right next to my head.

"I remember what happened next like it was a slow-mo dream. Passersby were frozen in mid-step. There wasn't another American in sight, no M.P.s and not even a White Mouse cop. And the Vietnamese avoiding me like ants around a stink bug, all looking the other way like they didn't care, it was none of their business.

"My attacker was young and skinny. He was wearing baggy gray short pants and a gray-green shirt. He looked like he might have been just out of high school. Of course, you can't really tell."

"Yeah, a full-grown Vietnamese dude won't weigh a hundred pounds soaking wet. Doesn't mean they can't kill you."

"I was finding that out. He shot at me again, and with that second shot he again missed high and to the same side. I saw the puff of smoke from the barrel of the revolver, heard the *chink* in the glass near my head, saw the look of anger and dismay when he realized he hadn't hit me."

"What did you do?"

"Honestly, Wild Bill, you'll think I'm crazy, but I just stood there, looking at him. I could have charged him, knocked him over and captured my very own VC terrorist."

"Or you could have got your ass shot off trying."

"Well, that's right. Or I could have ducked for cover, hit the deck. Or run away. To tell the truth, I didn't do any of those things. I was frozen in slow-mo, too. I didn't move a muscle, and, man, that was the longest few seconds of my life. I could see all the years I'd spent grinding through college, my mom and uncles and all the teachers who'd invested time and energy in me, all my hours of scribbling to become the next Hemingway, all that going to waste!"

"A guy is trying to kill you and you're thinking about writing a novel?"

Beale looked sad and frustrated. "I don't understand it to this day. I just stood there. He had all the time in the world. He tried another shot, but this time his gun jammed, or maybe he was out of bullets. My God, was he pissed, jabbering away at me! He was so upset he fell off his bike! And still, I did nothing. I probably could have taken him then, tackled him, wrested the revolver from his skinny little hand. I would have been a hero, the guy from the 3rd who actually caught a real live Viet Cong."

"Or, again, you could have rushed him and he'd have shot you point blank in the chest."

Beale's mind was a half-century away from their little table at the Starbucks in Beverly Hills.

"Maybe I didn't think of it. Maybe I wasn't hard-wired for aggression. Maybe nothing I'd learned in basic training had really stuck. It wasn't that I was frightened. I was a hard-scrabble kid from the wrong side of the tracks. I knew when to throw the brick and when to run. But at that moment, it seemed to me as clear as the vibration of a bell."

"What was clear?"

"I knew to the center of my being that the groove or whatever you call it — the channel of my luck — would hold steady so long as I did absolutely nothing at all."

"And you were right."

"Well, yes. The wannabe terrorist picked himself up, waving his pistol and yelling at me, 'De quoc xam luac my! De quoc xam luac my!' Invader-gangster American!

"He didn't expect it, but his revolver went off again, this wasted bullet firing into the air. And then he looked around, realized where he was and what he had in his hand."

Bill smiled. "I heard the Saigon special police made short work of terrorists. They attached copper electrodes to sensitive organs and expected answers to difficult questions."

"That had to be on his mind. He jumped back on his bike, frantically pedaled around the corner and was gone."

"Wow. Close call. What happened after that?"

"Comic relief. The manager of the leather goods store came out and yelled, '*Nguoi My sao!*' Ugly American."

"Right. Typical zip thinking. Somebody's got to pay for the window."

"Well, I'd had enough. There wasn't a White Mouse cop in sight. Or another American, either, for that matter. The pedestrians started to drift away. I thought about it. It was Saturday morning. I could see myself over at the Saigon police headquarters, staring blankly at endless mug shots. Then I would be escorted back to the 3rd, where I'd have to hear lectures about security from the C.O. After he finally let me go, I could drift over to the EMC club where grizzly sergeants would tell me what I should have done, and how they'd handled various krauts and gooks in hand-to-hand combat."

"Not how you'd planned your weekend with the lovely Therese."

"There I was, terrorist gone and what to do? Now that the danger was past, I was starting to feel reckless anger like hot metal rushing through my veins. I shouted at the shopkeeper, '*Nguoi Nam sao...* Ugly, yourself!'

"I took a last look at the bullet holes. They hadn't really been very close at all. The nearest one had clearly missed my head by over six inches. *'Sao. Sao lam. Sao nhut!'* I repeated, scoffing at the store manager with my finger, which, as you know, is a particular gesture of disrespect and scorn.

"I still had the package with my photo in it in my hand. I simply turned away and walked on down the street."

"Oh, oh. What did Therese think?"

"I tried to joke about it, but she didn't take my brush with the kid on the bike all that casually. After I calmed her down a little, we took off for Chez Brodard's without even waiting for one of her aunts to tag along.

"Bill, I guess you of all people understand how it is, sometimes, when the normal flow of things is upset. After the first thing happens, one thing seems to lead to another. Events can't be predicted or controlled. I had to go over everything that had happened, and it all seemed more or less okay until Therese broke down and started crying. I held her and stroked her silky black hair, but she just sobbed harder and harder.

"After that, I was at my wits end. I didn't know how to calm her down. I finally decided I had to tell her my theory of luck. She sobbed quietly while I explained how I was invincible, how nothing could get to me. I was in the groove of my luck, and so my luck was sure to hold. After all, I explained, I only had another two months and it was all over, anyway.

"She looked at me; I could see she was startled, like she was having a new awareness. Her voice was all quivery, 'What do you mean?'

"'It will be alright. Less than sixty days and I can go back to the real world where none of this is happening.'

'But...I thought you were here for a year. I thought all American G.I.s—?'

"'Yes, but I've already been here ten. Didn't you know that?'

"From the way her shoulders shook when she cried, I could see she didn't. After a time she grew quiet. She looked at me, a ray of hope in her expression.

"'Let's go away to Da Lat,' she suggested. 'Let's get out of this horrible city. A few days, a week if we can.'

"'Da Lat?!' That took me by surprise. I knew about Da Lat. It was an old French resort town, built in the highlands a hundred miles or so to the north so the Saigon elite could weekend out of the oppressive heat of the city. They had beautiful waterfalls and old colonial hotels. In the 1920s and '30s, before World War II, big international game hunters had dropped their wives off there, before disappearing into the rainforests in search of tigers and elephants.

"The words came tumbling out of her mouth in a rush, 'It is my favorite place in the entire world. My family has a house there. We could go there, just talk all this through. You would love Da Lat. It is so pretty there...'

"'How would we get there?'

'Air Vietnam goes twice a day.'

"'But I have a security clearance,' I blurted out. 'The Army won't let me go.'

'They won't have to know.'

"'But they would know. They know everything like that. They would stop me at the airport.'

'Well, we could get a driver...'

"It came to me in a rush, everything she was offering,

and what she was willing to give up.

"'But, Therese… but what about your big wedding in the Saigon Cathedral?'

"There were tears shining in the corners of her beautiful eyes, and her lip trembled.

'I don't care about that anymore,' she said.

"And then we were in each other's arms. Her lips were warm and I felt like dancing. God, for just a moment I hoped and wished and dreamed that this could go on forever. And then I opened my eyes. I don't know why I did that. It's always bad luck to open your eyes when kissing somebody. I never do it.

"Bill, to this day I don't know what it was. Maybe things were going along at too fast a pace. Maybe it was the rush of cold fear left over from my run-in with the shooter. I don't know what it was, but in that moment I saw that her eyes were open, too. Again, maybe it was nothing. Maybe they didn't have the eyes-shut-when-kissing rule in Vietnam. I didn't know. All I knew was that I felt uncomfortable, like I was physically too close to her. For the first time since I'd landed at Tan Son Nhut nearly a year before, I was feeling in my bones the distance I had come. I was half a world away from my home, my own culture and everything I had always known. I was in a land where people struggled for their identity and their very existence, where death stole almost casually into everyday life.

"Unpleasant ideas flashed through my overworked brain. The Vietnamese were a highly sophisticated race, bred to use their wits for survival. I remembered Ong Vung's stories from Monterey Language School, tales of

torture and revenge. Hai Ba Trung, the Two Trung
Sisters, who had freed the nation from the hated Chinese,
only to be forced to commit suicide upon the return of the
vengeful horde from the north. The strong man from the
village who had been forced by the VC to swallow his
bible after they convinced his mistress to betray him.
They rammed the holy book down his throat. All the
innocent kids whose parents had sent them off to
government schools against VC warnings, only to have
their writing hands chopped off as an example to others.
And then there was one of our own Vietnamese language
classmates, a Sergeant with a big family back in
Oklahoma, who was found floating in the Soc Trang River.
He'd gone fishing, ended up shot in the back of the head.
Even me, I'd had close calls before; I flashed back to the
night I'd tried to spend with a bargirl named Hoa in her
ramshackle one room apartment way out in one of the
unsecured suburbs, until I was alerted that they knew I
was there and were just waiting for the hand grenade to
arrive.   It all came back to me in a rush.

"And still, in that startling moment as insanely violent
images raced through my mind, my luck held. Even as I
looked into Therese's eyes, I had a sense of absolute
clarity, a moment of awareness when I could see the
future outlined before me as clearly as anything that had
ever happened to me in the past. And in that moment, I
saw murder, torture and death. I knew that, if we went to
Da Lat, something horrible would happen. I knew it in my
bones. I knew it in my blood. Whether we went by plane
or car, whether we stayed a day, a week or a month,
neither of us would survive.

"'I'll see if I can get the time off,' I said.

"But I had changed my tune too fast. She knew me too well. Even as I said it, we both knew we wouldn't be going up to the highlands together. I held her close for a few more minutes, and then said my farewells.

"It was nearly one, and I looked at my watch and told her I had to get back for the afternoon shift. I took a taxi to the main gate, and a cyclo-bus the rest of the way to Davis Station. Of course that was a lie, I didn't really have to go to work; I had the weekend off. I drifted over to the EMC club to see if the customary dose of scotch could calm down my hands enough so I could take them out of my pockets. The club was holding one of those randy and raucous shows; I remember there was a fuzzy sounding band and a round-eyed platinum blond with a whiskey-hoarse voice singing about meeting up with a girl on Wolverton mountain. At least the scotch was free. That was good, because I could see it was going to take a lot.

"For the rest of my tour, I went back to my old routine, hitting up the bars and the nightclubs. There was always some party at the villa, things going on, something to do. I didn't have any more incidents with terrorists; I tell you, I made my way that last two months right down the center of my luck. It is all luck, you know. I'm convinced that luck gets you through; or it doesn't... you know this yourself."

"And you never saw Therese again?"

"We met a few more times, those arranged lunches with an auntie tagging along, and even wrote her for a while after I got back.

"Once I was in the States, things were different. I

worked my way through the welcome-home-and-let's-get-smashed parties. I passed around the paintings and lacquered boxes and things I'd brought back for souvenirs. I got into the job hunting, looking for a cheap used car, settling in to my post-Army life. Those were exciting times — the Kennedy and King assassinations, the mounting anti-war protests, the civil rights movement in full bloom. Everybody was going to be a filmmaker, and I was caught up right in the middle of it."

"Those were the times, my friend." Wild Bill waved away the Starbucks girl. He got to his feet and stretched. "God, these achy old bones!"

Beale tossed down some tip money and joined him. As they made their way across the parking lot, a young kid came up to them and asked for their autographs. Beale took the frayed little book and signed *Jack Beale, Hollywood Director.* When Bill's turn came, he scrawled *John Wayne.*

The kid eyed him suspiciously, "John Wayne is dead."

Bill grinned and added *Jr.* after his signature and the kid ran off happy.

Beale stood by his BMW sportster. "Where you go now?"

"I have to take the bike back. Catch a plane. Buy an island."

"We ended up mostly talking about me."

"No, about Therese, actually. And I did ask."

"Odd how, even today, I remember her every now and again. That seems funny to you, I guess."

"No, it doesn't, Jack. Memories, you know?"

"Yeah, but that was such a long time ago, an entire

lifetime passed."

"Life goes on."

"Billy, she was just another girl I met along the way, and believe me, since then I've met my share."

"I bet you have, Mister Hollywood."

"I wonder why I should even think about her at all."

"Hey, be grateful we got through the mess."

"Yeah... I guess that's the way luck is. It gets you through the worst of times, but every once in a while, it leaves you with this handful of old images and emotions that for some reason will never entirely fade away."

"Yeah. That's just the way it is."

Wild Bill turned in his bike at the Harley place and told the sales guy he'd think about buying one. He was in a cab halfway to LAX when a thought struck him like a rifle butt to the head: Beale had been talking in code and the poor guy hadn't even realized it.

HOME FREE

June, 1965   His name is Beale. Jack Beale,
Specialist 5th Class. He's on his knees kissing the hot,
dusty tarmac at Travis Air Force Base when the balloon
splatters nearby. He hears a distant cheer, and jeers too.
And as he stands, he feels the warm, sticky red goo on his
face.

The sun is too hot for June in northern California, and
everything tilts a little bit from left to right, like he's back on
the My Canh floating restaurant and he's been drinking
too much Algerian Red. In the here and now he sees on
the other side of a cyclone fence, a motley, colorful knot of
young people. The girls are decked out in bright
headbands, and their short sexy skirts ride nearly up to
their crotches. The guys look grubby and unshaven.
They wear rumpled khaki, they sport V-finger buttons and
have the stars and stripes sewn on their butts. They laugh
in shrill excitement, encouraging the one with the
homemade sling to try again.

This guy named Beale is just a small-town kid from

Illinois who went to a small-time college in Indiana, and he's been away a while at a small-time war in southeast Asia. He stands there, dazed at the side of a runway at a military base in northern California. He doesn't understand what is happening.

The civilian contract airline people do their best to hustle Beale's little group along. As they begin their walk toward the low-slung, beige-colored military terminal, a burly Staff Sergeant mutters, "Goddamn filthy bastards..."

Beale, startled out of his reverie, looks over and reads "Morris" on the Sergeant's nameplate. He just stares as the Sergeant steps in close and tries to rub the smear off his face with the palm of his hand. It is an oddly gentle gesture for Sergeant Morris, a man used to the rough bark and cough of the military.

"What was that?" Beale asks, glancing back uneasily at the red stain on the asphalt.

"Goddamn pig's blood! Those filthy, mother-fucking motherfuckers!"

The Sergeant chokes on his rage, unable to articulate his feelings. He looks over his shoulder and angrily flails one hand, the fuck you finger up, gesturing at the protestors.

"Vietnam is nothing like they think," Beale manages to say, his voice coming out in that too-quiet way of his.

He takes another look over his own shoulder. By this time, the cops have arrived in a few olive squad cars and an M.P. is struggling with the balloon-flinger. Some of the kids are kicking and punching back, and Beale can see two civilian squad cars, still in the distance, approaching at high speed.

"Draft-dodging coward prick bastards," the Sergeant mutters angrily.

Beale is minutes back in The World after his tour in South Vietnam. He has had his wish; he has actually gone halfway around the world to see for himself the old, tortured, broken bones and flat, feverish, green skin of the place, and has returned alive and physically unharmed.

"You gonna be okay, Specialist?" someone asks. Beale snaps back to the present and he realizes the Sergeant named Morris still has him firmly by the elbow.

"Yeah. Why? I look bad?"

"You look... a little disconnected."

"I guess this wasn't the homecoming I'd imagined."

He moves away from the Sergeant and takes a seat in the deserted waiting area for gate 14. The rest of the de-planers file past and go on without him. He finds himself staring at nothing. His mind is on idle, spinning slowly a half a world away.

Beale is remembering a time early in his tour, a weekend evening, and he is wearing civvies. He's on a date with a slim but predatory bargirl. They are seated in one of Saigon's open-air cafes. The Catinat is a bar girl's favorite night-off haunt, and the place is crowded with servicemen in casual clothes and their *co gai* dolled up in their flashy finest – heavy makeup, spray-teased hair and skin-tight silk dresses. It's early evening, still too soon for the flares and the mortars to start up in the nearby countryside. It rained earlier, and now the neon lights from the Saigon bars and the traffic headlights are reflected in irregular pools of water that have gathered on the drenched cobblestone streets.

The G.I.s in Beale's unit have been encouraged to go downtown dressed as civilians so the VC will lose heart, knowing Uncle Sam is here to stay. At least, that's their theory. Beale is wearing an open-neck poplin shirt, a light cotton jacket and tan cotton pants, and there's a pipe and a small bag of smoking tobacco tucked in his shirt pocket. He hates sucking on the pipe but he's trying his best to look like a reporter or a novelist — anything but an Army enlisted man.

His date is young and desirable. Her name is Tuy. She thinks he might be a young Army officer, the ticket to her dreams. Beale met her at a crummy side-street bar near the main finger of one of the muddy estuaries running through the city. He knows what she thinks he is, so he plays the role. He puffs away at the cheap tobacco in his pipe and orders a bottle of red wine. The local government is putting the squeeze on the French; the wine turns out to be Algerian, bitter and expensive. Beale sips it like it is the most exquisite wine in southeast Asia. Tuy doesn't care; she chatters away in her broken English about Chanel No. 5 and Toni hairspray, and he settles in to watch the people passing by.

The big grenade scare has hit Saigon, but the Catinat still hasn't screened off their cafe. The rumor is they pay the Viet Cong so they can stay open without fear of a terrorist attack. The street on the other side of the waist-high wall is alive with peddlers, paperboys, Buddhist monks in orange robes and monk-novices in yellow or brown, pith-helmeted cyclo drivers, darting cabbies, fat White Mice cops with easy smiles, superior and arrogant ARVN Quoc Canh M.P.s, flashy whores, cute peanut girls, sly beggars, crutch-aided cripples, and even a low-flying flock of skateboarding lepers. Beale tries not to think about how easy it would be for anyone to toss in a grenade or a stick of dynamite.

Tuy is working the conversation around to the subject of Toni hairspray at the nearby American PX when an old hag sneaks into the cafe. This one is a typical begger-*ba*; bare-footed, ragged and filthy, with a wrinkled face and a pear-shaped body. She manages to slip by the bouncers and starts up the aisle, shaking and pinching her one-and-a-half-year-old baby and whining, "*Anh, Anh, Anh...*"

Her kid is an ugly half-American with sandy, reddish hair, olive skin and slanted eyes, and its angry cries fill the room.

The G.I.s mostly just look away, embarrassed and put-off, though Beale sees one guy start to put his hand in his pocket before his bargirl friend stops him. Bargirls don't like anybody tapping their personal gold mines, and they can be mean as snakes. Beale's theory is that they especially don't like beggar ladies, because it reminds them where they'll be in a few years once their youth and beauty hits the skids. A few of the girls start hazing the old lady, hissing at her and throwing things from their tables.

By this time, the old woman is right next to Beale, holding out the baby for his inspection. She shakes it and it howls like an angry cat. The open sores on its arms and legs are fresh and runny, and look like she's touched them up with sandpaper, the common practice among the beggar-moms who do this sort of thing.

Tuy can't take the interruption any more. She stands

up and yells, "*Di di, mau len,* Mamma-fucker!"

That's enough for the establishment. Two beefy Chinese guys catch the old *ba* under the arms and start to drag her away. A busty girl seated at one of the tables throws a pineapple square that hits the old lady in the center of the forehead and after that things go a little crazy. The old *ba* screams through her blackened, broken teeth and jerks free long enough to spit a huge gob of bright orange betelnut juice in the center of the busty girl's pink silk cocktail dress. Too late now, the bouncers fling the old lady, still clutching her meal-ticket kid, outside onto the sidewalk in the general direction of one of those French-style Erector Set telephone posts. She tries to use the baby as a cushion, but they both hit the rusty, paint-flaked metal frame pretty hard and she looks woozy as she jumps to her feet and swings around, still yelling and shaking the kid at her hecklers like a little live voodoo idol.

There is no room for pity among the girls who ply their wares in the bars of downtown Saigon, and the old *ba* is met with a new volley of curses and flying food. She steps back; her foot twists on the curb and she goes down, falling backwards into the street. The baby's wail and her own high-pitched voice are cut short under the wheels of a big, olive colored deuce-and-a-half with a white star stenciled on the side. There's a popping sound, far more horrible than those the balloons made on the tarmac at Travis, and while their severed bodies still shudder and dance, the baby and the beggar-lady's heads are just a red-and-gray smear on the cobblestones.

"Oh, for Christ Jesus sake!" Tuy snarls.

Beale gags and spills his cheap wine on the linen

tablecloth. He has the presence of mind to scatter money on the table and to pull Tuy away before the M.P.s arrive.

Nothing bothers Tuy. As their cab scoots across town, she questions Beale about Debby Reynald's hairstyle in the movie 'Tammy' and wonders at Elizabeth Taylor's use of eye-liner in 'Cleopatra.' Their driver stops in front of a narrow, unlit street. In spite of Tuy's sharp commands, he refuses to drive any further; he reaches around to grasp Beale's arm and gives him a warning look. It's a borderline VC area and Beale is feeling rotten anyway, so he promises Tuy a wonderful cosmetics expedition and sends her on her way. Then he slouches in the back seat while the battered blue-and-cream Renault putters through the rain back to the *Tan Son Nhut* airbase.

That's his first real taste of Vietnam. Welcome to big time pearl of the orient, G.I. As the days tick by, he gradually comes to believe survival is a matter of timing. There's a mortar attack, explosions stalking across the runway to end in the barracks next door to where he is hiding under his bunk bed. They take fire from the tree line, just a few sniper shots, but enough to send the guys from his barracks running and diving for cover. One night there's a Buddhist riot, rumors of an anti-American gang stuffed with hate and armed with hatchets and shotguns, swelling the streets and supposedly heading for the air base where he is stationed.

The string of unpleasantness extends itself while, at the same time, bit by bit by bit, Beale himself slowly comes unraveled, like an old-fashioned Midwestern quilt coming undone with the haphazard punch and slap of everyday living. He becomes intentionally unpredictable; he relies more and more on hunches, omens, and finally, his lucky lullaby. One day, he has to finish one last little two-sentence decode before lunch, and so he misses the Airport Restaurant bombing that takes out his First Sergeant and a dozen other Americans. He visits Old Sarge at Saigon General before they ship him back to the PI. Sarge's skin is all pepper-potted from cement fragments; his eyes are crossed like a cartoon goon and his hearing is half-gone.

"I'll be back," Sarge mumbles from his drug-heavy stupor.

Behind Sarge's back, an orderly dressed in neat whites shakes his head in the negative.

"Lucky to be alive," the orderly whispers to Beale.

The next day, Beale sees a black cat and he completely changes the way he walks to work. He knows there are no stray cats in Saigon. The Vietnamese eat cats.

Beale's days and nights are occupied with his job and with the endless round of Army details. He doesn't have any close friends. Nobody notices anything different about him, or if they do, they don't say.

The days and weeks tick by, and Beale's luck holds, and holds and holds. He is two minutes away from the U.S.O. on Saigon's famous "Street of Flowers" when a car bomb with over 100 kilos of *ep plastique* blows, digging a six foot hole in front of the U.S. Embassy and splattering car fenders, arms, legs and warm, wet guts over a crowded city block. Another time, over on Le Loi Street, a kid on a motorbike actually fires three rounds at him from twenty feet away. The bullets break the plate glass window in a luxury leather shop behind his head. The bike spills, the kid gets up, pistol still in his hand. He stares for a long, crazy moment at Beale before he panics and scrambles away. The shop owner comes out and yells at Beale to pay for his window.

The moment fades...

Sitting alone in the waiting room at Travis, Beale knows it is all behind him now, just a bunch of old war stories. The problem is, they are his stories, and they arch like mortar rounds in his head, looming like monstrous red cannonballs until they spatter against the walls, the floors, the ceiling.

A signal bongs on the intercom and when Beale hears that hollow sound, he's back in Saigon again. He knows that sound — it is the sound of a short two-by-four bat connecting with a wispy village elder's head. The old guy is down and the swarming Saigon Cowboys are laughing like barking dogs. The scene shifts and Beale's walking along Nguyen Hue Street, less than a half-hour after the car bomb went off. He looks up and sees yellow-gray intestines hanging from a tree branch and he wonders who gets the job of cleaning up. He knows very well there is always someone who cleans up. You can't leave guts in a tree, he tells himself. He walks on, stops in wonder. He is staring down at a little Vietnamese foot in a blue tennis shoe that is lying on the ground with nobody connected to it. He hurries on past, wondering how such a thing is overlooked. Shift to the med-center at *Tan Son Nhut* and the side-gunner moans and turns on his pallet and Beale sees his jaw is gone, shot entirely away.

"What do you want?" the med-center nurse asks Beale.
He dumbly shakes his head and leaves, ashamed to tell
her aspirin.

The red balloons bulge and spatter again and again,
and there is nothing Beale can do. He sits alone in the
air-conditioned lobby at Travis for almost an hour and he
sees that the pig's blood is everywhere, on the floors, the
walls, even the ceiling. There's a spatter on his tie. He
wonders how the Sergeant could have missed it.

Finally, a young hostess comes over.

"You've got to check-in now, sir," she says. "Everyone
in your group has gone on ahead."

Beale sees she has a bloody, irregular blotch on her
jacket, and more blood on her shoes. She talks to him,
but he isn't fooled, because he recognizes her jabber for
that same cheery airline way they all have.

He goes along with her without saying anything, and
she leads him to the check-in place. She pretends the
whole time that she doesn't mind how messy she looks,
like the blood isn't really there. *That takes discipline,* he
whispers to himself.

"It's nothing like they think," he says in a louder voice,
still trying to ignore the blood, which is everywhere,
dripping off of everything.

"I'm sure it isn't, sir," a polite young man behind the
counter replies in that same chipper tone. As he reaches
for Beale's papers, Beale notices he has a stain, too, a
damp scarlet spot on his shirt, mostly hidden by his jacket.
Beale sighs and pulls at his collar. It seems best not to
mention that spot, either.

With the physicals and everything, it takes Beale four

days to muster out of the Army. Finally, they've given him the last talk, the final papers, his honorable discharge and a pat on the back, and sent him on his way. He stands on the curb outside the base entrance. It's just past sunset, with the flavor of the setting sun still in the far western sky. He thinks about the sun, out over the Pacific, moving in the direction of the South China Sea. Beale is now wearing new civvies, a neat pair of light green slacks and a dark green polo shirt with a maroon wool sweater around his shoulders. His duffle bag lies nearby on the ground, stuffed with the new clothes he's bought at the PX, the clothes he's going to wear in his new life.

The Army life is behind him now. He's done his time. He is no longer Jack Beale, Specialist Fifth Class. He is a civilian. He sucks in a deep breath of the cool evening air and then waves his thumb in the general direction of Sacramento. No luck for a while. He sees that somewhere on the other side of the high concrete block fences, the Rainbird sprinklers are making their intermittent hissing noise, lofting their misty spray over parched summer lawns. Out by the road where he is standing, there is just a swift and quiet little stream of water runoff shooting along the curb.

After a few minutes, some Yay-hoos in a VW bus with flowers painted on the side come chugging smartly along. The driver notices Beale's duffle bag, and laughs and jerks his steering wheel with a quick move. Beale sees the van swerve toward him in time to jump back, but a chilling sheet of spray shoots over his pants legs.

Beale looks after the VW, now roaring off into the distance. He doesn't shake his fist or pass the finger of fury. Instead, he fondles the big Gerber switchblade in his pocket and calmly wonders how the Yay-hoo and his pals would like it if he slit their throats and threw balloons filled with their blood at people he didn't like. Beale looks down at his pants. The pig's blood clings there, crimson in the fading light. He brushes the droplets off with a little shudder, humming his lucky Bay La Song, the simple old Vietnamese lullaby that an ancient laundry-*ba* sang early that morning after the VC mortared three of his buddies into red mush from the tree line.

He pushes out his thumb at the next approaching car, still singing softly to himself, "Bay la, la, Bay la la, Bay la... Bay la, la, Bay la, la, Bay la..."

Beale has made it back from hell. He's alive and in one piece and he's only 24 years old. He's free, free, *freeeeeeeee*... free as a young songbird, wings outstretched with the rest of his life in front of him.

ABOUT JOHN KLAWITTER

After signing up for three years in the U.S. Army, his first civilian job was that of junior copywriter at a famous advertising agency where a highly paid Creative Director declared John Klawitter to be 'the most undirect-ible person he ever met.' A few months later John won an EMMY award for a documentary he created with world-famous Artist Reporter Franklin McMahon, Sr.

In the decades since, John Klawitter has created successful films and videos for major agencies and for most of the Hollywood studios, including Disney, Warner Bros, Universal, Paramount, and Hanna-Barbera, working with such legends as Ray Bradbury, Rod Serling, Orson Wells, Leslie Nielson, Arthur Pierson, Art Babbett, Bill Hanna, Joe Barbera, Bugs Bunny and Goofy. (How many directors can say they actually directed Goofy?)

Relying on his tinseltown experiences, John Klawitter has written eight novels and six non-fiction books. In 2009 he was a double winner: his novel **Hollywood Havoc** won an Epic Author's award for Best Action Thriller, and his non-fiction book **Tinsel Wilderness** won Best Non-Fiction Book. For more information see his website at www.johnklawitter.com

www.ingramcontent.com/pod-product-compliance
Lightning Source LLC
Chambersburg PA
CBHW050934120626
46552CB00001B/202

* 9 7 8 1 9 3 8 6 7 4 0 7 5 *